BROKEN EDGE

The Edge - Book Three

CD REISS

Broken Edge
CD Reiss
The Edge - Book Three
© 2018 Flip City Media Inc.
All rights reserved.
Print ISBN - 978-1-718831-09-4

If any person or event in this book seems too real to be true, it's luck,
happy coincidence, or wish-fulfillment on the reader's part.

Part One

CRACKING

STOP

If you haven't read the FREE prequel yet, you should do that before reading this book.

GET THE **FREE** PREQUEL
—— *CUTTING EDGE* ——

Chapter One

NEW YORK
MARCH 2007

Before he left, he made sure I was set. Here was the property tax bill. Anthony would pay it when he paid the utilities. Here was the water filter system. It needed to be changed in six weeks. He'd have called Franco to do it, but the number was on the—

"You can't go."

We were in the laundry room. Its base functionality seemed absurd against the backdrop of my husband going to war. How dare the washing machine be white when this was happening. Fuck you, dryer, for being half an inch higher. The basket of clothespins was a slap in the face, and the steady hush of the water heater was a mockery.

Caden looked green in the fluorescent light, and his eyes were flat gray. He looked as if he were dead already. "I knew I could get called."

"You were tricked."

He smiled ruefully. Even green, he was beautiful. Too brilliant to be conned, too loyal to go back on a promise. He put his hands on my shoulders and slid them down to my biceps. "I'm going to be fine. They're giving me a nice bonus."

"Because I care about money."

The smile went from rueful to pleased, and I had to admit he'd been more himself in the past day than he'd been since his alter ego had appeared.

"Did you tell them about Damon?"

"I took a battery of tests."

"They'd never send you if they knew."

"As soon as I read that letter, as soon as *he* read it, he crawled back into the hole he came from."

"He's gone?"

"Are you going to miss him?" he teased.

"Are you?"

"If I deploy, he's staying gone." He gathered my hands in his. "I won't miss the little chickenshit."

"He's the cowardly side of you."

He got close to my face and put up his finger. "I don't have a cowardly side."

The way he looked at me, I could kind of believe it. He was so strong, so clear, so commanding, even with a part of him stuffed into a dark bag. If I hadn't known better, I would have forgotten to worry about him. I would have overlooked the broken pieces for the sake of seeing the man in front of me.

"We all have a coward in us," I said.

"You don't."

"I do. She's scared of heights and spiders. And she's so scared of losing you."

He took my chin and pointed it up to face him. "I see that look on your face, Major."

"What look, Major?" I had to smile at our equal footing.

"You are not to walk into the AMEDD recruiter."

"I was going to stay in the military for life anyway. It's easy for me. We can get a dual deployment. They'll station us together."

"Maybe. Or they can put us half a world apart."

"It's a risk, but I'm willing to take it."

"I'm not willing." He put my hands against his chest. "You're going to run the PTSD unit of Mt. Sinai

Hospital. You're going to do what you were meant to do with your life. Help people after they get back. All you'd do on active duty is manage to get a revolving door of soldiers honorable discharges. They'd come back fucked up with no one to help them because you're on the other side of the wall."

I looked away from him at the way our hands wove together against his chest. "You think a lot of me."

"The world needs you."

"What about you? Do you need me?"

He unwove our fingers and put his arms around me, squeezing me so tightly it hurt.

"I need you," he said with his mouth pressed to my scalp, inhaling the scent of my panic. "I need you safe. I need you here. I'm a selfish and greedy man. I need you to stay here and do your work so I can keep it together. You're the only thing in this world saving me from going insane."

"What if he comes back?"

"He won't."

"He will."

"Well, then they'll send me home in disgrace. Maybe he'll buy a Maserati to make it up to you." He pulled away enough to meet my gaze. "But if you're deployed, you won't be here to make him sell the Ferrari first."

I laughed. He smiled with me, brushing a ribbon of hair off my cheek.

"I'm going to drive it when you're gone."

"Drive it now." He closed the panel door of the water filtration unit. "It's got a lot of kick."

"You're almost back to your old self."

"I think he needed a shock to the system. He's terrified of going back, and when the letter came, he wanted no part of it." Shrug. "War is his limit."

"You were forced to face your worst fear."

I saw his sharp glance behind me, to the false safe. The door was closed, but behind it was the bottle room and a darkness that had its own density. He looked back at me, his stare hard and locked as if he wanted to make sure I was there.

"Definitely the worst," he said, grabbing me and pulling me to him. "I can handle anything now." He kissed me, and I moved with him as he pressed his growing erection against me.

"We have about twenty-four hours," I said. "Can we spend twenty of them fucking?"

"What are we wasting those four hours on?"

"Sleep?"

He picked me up. I wrapped my legs around his waist.

"You'll sleep when you're dead."

We kissed as he carried me, clanking and banging ankles and elbows, kissing between ows and ouches, laughing all the way up the stairs. We wound up rolling on the carpet between the back door and the door to my office, peeling off as much of our clothing as we needed to get his dick inside me.

I braced each foot against an opposing wall as he pushed into me until he hit the end, and with another thrust, he found my limit but kept pushing.

Yes, it hurt. And yes, he knew it.

He did it again, and while he was buried deep, he yanked up my shirt and bra.

"I'm going to miss these tits," he growled right before getting his mouth under one and sucking the skin, closing his teeth against the flesh in a long, painful bite.

I fisted his hair, pulling his mouth against me, begging for the hurt. He bit and sucked, thrusting hard and slow, rotating his hips when he was rooted in me.

"I love you," I cried when I was close. "Caden, I love you."

In response, he bit me harder, and I came right into the pain.

Chapter Two

CADEN

Greyson passed out at one in the morning after I'd bathed her, laid her on the clean sheets, and taken another of her orgasms. She was sore. I could taste the raw skin when I licked her cunt, sharp with open nerve endings and the threat of blood.

But I couldn't sleep for the allotted four hours. There was too much to do. As I went about preparing the house for my absence and making Greyson's world as easy as possible without me, I felt as right as I had in a while. At least as right as I'd felt since Damon had ruptured my mind.

He was in the corners again, but I knew what he was now. He was my fear. He'd always been there, and when I faced him, he went away. My relief didn't last. Neither did my control.

Damon fled at the thought of war and danger, but

something else had been born. It didn't hum in the white noise. It was a hard buzz, like the approach of hornets. I told myself it was just Damon and I had him in hand, but it wasn't. I knew it, and I decided not to know it at the same time.

I went back into the laundry room to check on the circuit breakers. I'd be gone a couple of summers. The HVAC unit that had been installed while Greyson was still deployed was newer than the electrical box.

With a roll of tape around my wrist and a felt-tip pen behind my ear, I opened the metal panel. The black switches were labeled with masking tape in my father's handwriting, and since the new unit had been installed, many of them were wrong. I knew which was which and had never bothered correcting them.

I'd talk her out of selling the house for now. I wanted her to have a place to live in or sell if something happened to me. I'd pitch her the idea that since I wasn't here, there was no need to worry about me getting triggered by the fucking moldings or whatever she thought had prompted my split. We could sell when I got back.

Peeling off the first swatch of masking tape, I realized how neat my father's writing had been. He'd made a lie of the cliché about doctors having sloppy handwriting. He'd made a lie out of a lot of expectations.

I ripped off a piece of tape and put it by the switch. My edge was straight but ragged from the tear. My father had used scissors, of course. And when I wrote "Dining Room" on the tape and it was a mess, I realized he'd written the label while it was still flat on the roll.

I peeled it off and started over.

NEW YORK
1981

TWO PAIRS OF SCISSORS.

My favorite T-shirt.

My most recent algebra test.

Three pages torn from an old *Hustler* magazine.

The shirt was still crisply black, and the three digitally-styled symbols, one for each band member in the Police, were still alarm-clock red. It was laid out on the shiny dining room table without a wrinkle.

My algebra test was lined up parallel to the edge of the table.

The *Hustler* nudes were spread above that, pages creased, with corners curling and the pinkest parts faded with age.

Dad sat at the head of the table. When I saw my mother

kneeling at his feet, I dropped my bag. It was open. A pencil rolled out.

"How old are you, Caden?" my father asked as if he'd ever forget the day the mess was born.

"Eleven, sir." I tried to make eye contact with Mom, but she was bent toward the Persian carpet.

"Come here."

I stepped toward him, close enough to hear my mother's ragged breaths, and with the new angle, I could see that he held the end of a belt. The other end was looped around Mommy's neck.

"Describe what's on this table."

I took my gaze away from my mother and looked at the table. "Two pairs of scissors. My *Ghost in the Machine* shirt. My algebra test. Three—"

"More on the test, please. Finish the job."

Mom coughed. I started to sweat. He wanted me to be specific, and I needed to pay attention.

"It's from last week. Wednesday. There's an eighty-six in red at the top, and under it is the word 'good' in script with an exclamation point. The magazine—"

"You're not finished with the test. What's in the left corner?"

"Your signature, sir."

Mom gasped. I couldn't look. I couldn't watch him making the belt tighter, and I knew he wanted me to keep my eyes on the table.

"Did I make that signature?"

"No, sir."

"Who did?"

"I did, sir."

"Why did you do that? And be honest, please. I don't want this to be harder than it has to be."

"I thought you'd get mad that it was a low grade."

"I would get mad. I didn't fight for you to be in eighth grade math so you could get fourteen percent of the questions wrong, did I?"

"No, sir."

"And what about the magazine? Where would an eleven-year-old boy get pictures like that?"

"Brian Muldoon's brother." Brian was Irish. He had six brothers and sisters. The *Hustler* was a third-generation hand-me-down.

"All the Irish do is fuck and have babies, Caden. Don't forget it."

"Yes, sir."

"Can you tell me what you think you're looking at?"

If I hadn't been sweating before, I was when he asked me to study the photos.

"A motorcycle." Mom heaved a breath. I was shaking. "A naked lady on a motorcycle."

"What's she doing?"

"Showing her... thing."

He yanked Mom up to her knees. Her hands clutched the belt, and her eyes tried to tell me everything was all right.

"Your mother was hiding these with the test when I came home. Do you think she'd bother hiding a meaningless *thing*?"

"No. Yes? I... I don't know."

"Don't know what? The real name?"

He must have wanted me to not call it a "thing."

"Puh-puh-pussy."

"No." He denied my answer, but it satisfied him enough to let Mom back to the floor. "These 'things' have *names*."

I swallowed. My mother didn't make a sound. Her silence was for me. I was old enough to know that but too young to forgive her for it.

"Vulva," I whispered.

"Louder. Like a man."

"Labia minora."

"Better."

"Labia majora." Tears streamed down my face, but I spoke clearly around the sobs. "Urethral meatus. Clitoris. Vestibule. Introitus."

"Very good. You're qualified for a career in gynecology. Now. You have two pairs of scissors. One is for fabric. One is for paper. Cutting paper with fabric scissors dulls them. Paper scissors cut fabric inefficiently. You use the right tool for the right job. When you're done, your mother will start dinner."

I picked up the heavy fabric scissors and sliced my favorite shirt in half. After I'd shredded it to rags, I switched scissors and started on the test. Last, I cut up the motorcycles and the women on them, hoping he wouldn't notice that I'd left their delicate parts intact. I couldn't bear to slice those. It hurt to think about.

When I was finished, I was sent into the bottle room until Mom finished making dinner.

NEW YORK
MARCH 2007

"YOU STILL LOOK REALLY SEXY in dull green,"

Greyson said with a wry smile, placing her hands on my shirt.

I wasn't the only service member stalling by the entrance to security. A quick count of men and women in uniform came to eight, and I would have put ten on all of them going to North Carolina. I didn't know them, but we nodded to each other. We were each one of a number adding up to an escalation.

"I don't want you to worry," I said, drawing her close.

"I won't."

"You're a terrible liar."

"If it happens... if Damon comes back..."

"He won't. Not while I'm there. After that... I don't know."

The security line was getting ridiculous even as we stood there.

"Maybe we'll just move to the Middle East after the war. I hear the Green Zone's sorta nice."

"Sure."

An agent in a striped scarf and polyester vest moved a velvet rope and flipped a sign, opening a special line for military personnel.

"That's you." Her eyes were glassy. Tears would drop at the next blink.

"Listen to me," I said. "I know we've had a hard run. This marriage hasn't been what you wanted, and it hasn't been what I expected. But I think we didn't want or expect enough. We're bigger than that. We thought we'd be normal, but we aren't normal."

She blinked and tightened her lips into a line. I kissed the salty tears that fell down her cheeks.

"I won't miss you," I whispered. "Because you'll be with me. You were always with me. We're not bound by some vows we made in your parents' backyard. Those promises were for the rest of the world to hear, but between us? It's older. Bigger. My cells are tied to yours. Remember I told you that when we met, I couldn't explain the feeling to myself? I didn't have a worldview big enough to fit what you were in my life. You were *already there*. And when I think I won't be able to handle... whatever it is, I know you're still there. Your strength keeps me upright when I think I'll fall. I can't shake you or forget you, because you run through my veins."

"Like an infection."

"Like a nutrient. Vitamin G, baby."

She laughed through her tears, wiping them away with her wrist. Around us, children waved good-bye to mothers and fathers as they passed the civilians in line.

"We were always *us*," Greyson said. "That feels right."

"Hold that feeling."

"You hold it too."

I kissed her lips as the last of the stalling military personnel wove through the maze of ropes.

"Go." She pushed me away. "Go before I cling to your pant leg."

One more kiss, then I picked up my duffel. I looked back one more time before I turned to get on line. That buzz that no one else heard was deep in the airport's noise. It sounded as if I was walking into a hornets' nest.

"Wait!" my wife cried, digging into her bag.

I stopped, waited, relieved for a moment's grace from the swarm in security. She handed something across the rail between us.

The rabbit's foot.

"For your expanded worldview."

With the rope separating those leaving from those staying pressed to my gut, I kissed her so deeply we knotted the ancient tie that held us together.

Chapter Three

GREYSON

I kept walking around the house.

I'd seen him off to a week of training in Fort Bragg, after which he'd be sent to Iraq as part of the troop surge. He'd kissed me at JFK, and I'd breathed him deeply, smelling fresh coffee grounds and the laundry detergent we'd washed his uniform in. The taste of my pussy was faint on his tongue, but once he brushed his teeth and showered, I'd be erased from his body despite his claims of a marital vascular infection. Vitamin G.

He'd said a lot of things in our last day together, and I believed he'd meant every word. When I stopped overthinking everything, in the nether state where wakefulness won't leave and sleep won't come, I knew they were all true. He and I were bound together by something more than shared history and compatible pheromones.

I knew him. My instincts felt his presence in the world. He'd meant what he said, but he was torn apart. Pulled away from his feelings, his passions, his doubts. Damon had been forced back into the bag, along with half of what I loved about him.

And his feelings for me? They were locked away even if he said they weren't. I was a feeling he knew he was supposed to have, a love he believed he had but didn't understand.

Without him in it, the brownstone was a fancy hotel. I smelled him in the sheets, in the shirts hanging in the closet. His love was in the furniture choices in my office, soaked in the linens, in the things I liked that he'd left for me in the refrigerator. But soon, those things would be gone.

I walked the house in the dark, exploring closets and corners built in 1821 and saturated with the aches and triumphs of the five families that had owned it. In an unused room on the top floor, a window seat held a stash of old *New York Times* from World War I. The brown paper flaked to the touch, and the pictures were muddled, grainy blobs inside rectangles. I tried to read them, but without the exhausting detachment I showed at work, I couldn't concentrate. There was no point anyway.

Different time. Different war. Different soldier.

I threw the papers back and wandered again, looking for

answers to questions I couldn't articulate. Loneliness and loss weren't wandered away.

I ended up in the bottle room. It was bare, flat concrete down to the corners.

I shut off the light and closed the door. The darkness was complete. Heavy. Thick. It partnered with the silence to press against the senses.

Feeling for the wall, I leaned against it, crouching to the floor. Nothing to see, hear, taste, smell. I touched the cold floor to get a sense of my space and reality.

The compulsion to leave was so strong I sucked in a breath and stood without willing myself to. That deep breath, coming after the smell of nothing, brought a new scent so faint it would have disappeared in any other room.

Copper. Iron. Meat. An operating room without the sting of cleansers.

Blood. It was blood.

I turned on the light and inspected the floor. It was spotless.

Eventually, I gave up and went back into the laundry room, where I smelled nothing but fabric softener and dust.

He was landing in Fort Bragg, and I was desperately worried.

"LOOK," the AMEDD recruiter said. I'd finally called. It was the same guy who'd signed him the first time. "Anyone who's been on a previous deployment gets a battery of psych testing. If he passes, he goes."

"What tests? Specifically."

"ASVAB, TAPAS, MEPS. MMPI for meds. Plus an interview. If he had PTSD, we would have caught it."

"Are you sure?"

"Trust us. We've done this before."

And that was that. Caden was going to do what he did, and the army would do what it did. It was out of my hands.

Soon after I hung up and went upstairs, the phone rang. It was our first night apart. Had Damon punctured the curtain that detached the doctor from the man? Had he freaked out? Was the call from Command telling me to come get this un-soldierly mess?

I ran down the stairs like a woman on fire.

"Honey?"

My mother.

"Mom?"

"Why didn't you tell me?"

I stared into the sink. It was bone-dry. "I don't know."

I knew, but it was too awful a reason. I hadn't wanted to tell her I'd lost. My battle to not be like her had been won only briefly. In the end, my husband had gone away and left me home to worry and wait.

"Your father says it'll be fine."

"When did he get back?"

"It'll be fine!" Dad called from the background.

"Welcome home!" I exclaimed. He'd been in Japan.

"He's back, and he says—"

My father's brusque voice came on the line. "He's a doctor. He's not getting shot at."

"I'm not worried about him dying, Dad." I regretted saying that before I was done with the sentence. They'd ask what I *was* worried about.

Thankfully, my father had a point to make that superseded mine.

"Besides," he continued as if I hadn't said anything. "It's not like it was. Now it's all tactical strikes. It's not as messy."

Sure. A clean war. Because if a foreign army came down Main Street, USA, in an orderly fashion, everyone would be calm and the battles would be bloodless.

"He'll be fine." I leaned over the counter, flicking a grain of sugar off the marble.

With a click, my mom got on the other line. "You should come stay with us."

"She has an important job now, Louise."

"Then I can go there." Mom sounded as if she'd tried to make this point a few dozen times.

"I'm fine," I said. "Really. Maybe I'll come out for a weekend."

"Bring your brother," Dad huffed.

"Charles," my mother said, "I'd like to speak to my daughter."

"About what?"

I smiled and rubbed my eyes. My persistence had been handed down in my genes.

"Woman talk."

Dad grunted and hung up the phone.

"Mom, I'm fine."

"I know you are. I'm not worried about *you*. I'm never worried about you. It's Caden. You always said he was a civilian in uniform."

I bristled. I was allowed to say and think that, but I didn't want to hear it from anyone else. "He's more than qualified, and if you'd seen him in Fallujah, you'd know that."

"Yes, I understand."

I could almost hear her smile, and I knew why. I was being unreasonably defensive, and she knew it. I sounded like a loyal army wife, which I'd become in spite of all my efforts.

"But, yeah, I'm having a hard time."

"Come home for a weekend," she said. "We can talk."

Chapter Four

THE GREEN ZONE
BAGHDAD
APRIL 2007

Baghdad was different from Balad and much the same as I remembered from Greyson's injury three years before. The facilities were permanent. I had a room, not a trailer. The docs shared a personal computer with spotty, expensive Wi-Fi. I'd been inserted into an established unit as a replacement, and I hadn't even met my new CO before I heard the first of two Blackhawks drop onto the landing pad.

The buzz dispersed like hornets in a high wind.

And suddenly, I knew what I was doing. A butterbar who went by the unexplained nickname "Toadie" was showing me around when I heard the *thup-thup* of rotors.

I must have snapped to attention like a man waking up from sleep.

"It's all right," he said. "We're staffed."

"I want to see triage."

EIGHT AT ONCE. IED. The madness and noise of triage had an orderly pattern. Toadie fell away into his own job as I entered into mine, following the last injured man. He was gurgling. Color was bad.

"St. John. 61J." I gave the medic the code for general surgeon. "What do we have?"

"IED. Fucking mess. Chest wound. Lungs filling up."

She gave me his vitals as I opened his shirt. Fucking mess was right, but I'd managed worse in poorer conditions.

"Get him prepped for the OR."

"Hey, what are you doing here?" Male voice from behind.

I turned. White guy in scrubs. Six-three. Bald head shaped like a wedge. I stuck out my hand. "Cap—Major St. John. I'm your new GS."

He shook. "Captain Quinn. Ortho. Call me Boner. Glad to have you. Scrub-in is third on the right." As I walked down the hall, Boner called, "Six tonight!"

I turned and walked backward.

He continued. "The roof. Thursday is Beerday."

I gave him the thumbs-up.

I PUSHED into the scrub room. Three surgeons were getting their blues on over their clothes. The fourth was in the process of stripping off a blood-soaked uniform. When she saw me, she paused, clearly unashamed of her mismatched bra and panties.

"You must be the new 61J," she said, hands on the curve of her hips, ignoring the nurse who held out a gown for her.

She was daring me to look at her body, so I didn't. I stayed focused on her ochre eyes. "St. John. Caden."

She held her hands out for the gown. "I hope you live longer than the guy you're replacing." She turned around to give the nurse access to the back of the gown.

"Lt. Cash," a female nurse introduced herself. "Call me Aretha. Sink's here..." She quickly showed me the layout of the room, and I got to work.

I tried not to think about how the last guy had exited his job. If I died in Iraq, Greyson would find a way to bring me back to life so she could personally kill me.

Thinking about her raging doggedness, I couldn't help but smile.

Even with thousands of miles between us, her tenacity made me strong.

I FELT GOOD, working on that first chest wound. In control. Sane, mostly. I knew sanity was a slippery concept, but Damon was gone, replaced by a buzz I didn't know well enough to fear. I didn't have time to attribute it to the pace of the work or even pure necessity. I only had time to get pieces of metal from a guy's lungs.

"Need help?" Female voice.

I looked up. It was the half-naked woman from the changing room.

"Almost done."

"How's his love muscle?" I must have reacted because she smiled under her mask. "His heart."

"Little nick right here." I pointed. "We got it in time."

"Good find." She met my gaze over the table. "Those are some pretty eyes you have there."

"Thanks." I put my attention back on the patient. "Got them from my father."

"He must be a handsome guy."

"He was an asshole, if that matters."

To my relief, she walked away without answering.

THE DOCS HAD SET up chairs in front of the rooftop stairway structure. A thick layer of clouds hung over the sky. At Boner's feet sat a specimen cooler full of half-warm beer cans. A doc with a flat top and a diamond earring on the left handed me a can.

"This is Captain Jackson," Boner said.

"Call me Stoneface."

"Thanks." I took the can of Miller Lite and shook his hand.

"Major McDonnell over here. He's a fucking star."

As I shook the hand of the man with curly red hair and boyish cheeks, McDonnell said, "Agent Orange. And I'm no star."

"You guys and the names." I cracked the can and tried to catch the foam before it made a mess.

Without warning, the air was filled with a plaintive voice singing in Arabic. It came from a thin stone tower that rose above the rest of the city. The voice hopped from octave to octave, calling all Muslims in earshot to prayer.

"You get used to it." Another white guy with an all-

American haircut and clean cheeks transferred his O'Doul's to his left hand so he could hold his right out to me. "I'm Timothy Eberhardt."

"Let me guess yours," I said as I shook. "Boy Scout?"

"Good guess, but it's Heartland."

"Nice one. Who gives these out? So I can avoid them."

"Harpy," Boner said. "Our CO."

"Harpy?"

"Colonel DeLeon," Jackson said. "She's all right. You'll like her."

"I think I met her in the OR." I wasn't shocked or dismayed that a woman was running the unit. I wasn't concerned with *what* she was but *who* she was.

"Smart mouth?" Eagle asked. "Light-brown hair with eyes to match?"

"Body like a—" Agent Orange stopped himself and sipped his beer.

"Yeah. That's her."

"A real firecracker," Heartland said.

"She'd get along great with my wife," I offered. "Same set of brass balls."

I loved Greyson's balls, and truth be told, I loved bragging about them.

"Where's she holding the fort down from?"

"New York."

"Civilian?"

"Resigned her commission last year," I answered. "But she's from a long line of military, so she gets it. Her father was in the 101st Airborne. Plane jumper."

"Badass." Stoneface tipped his beer in respect. "Mine's military too. She's nearly snapped my neck between her thighs a few times."

"Probably because you eat pussy like a dog lapping a bowl of water," Boner said.

"What do you know about pussy, cocksucker?"

"Spread your legs, and I'll show you."

We all laughed at the final insult. Boner and Stoneface tapped their cans and drank.

The singing stopped, leaving the whipping wind to fill the soundscape.

It was there. The buzzing. The new Thing.

I heard it in the white noise, breathing in my ear like an angry parent. Not weak like Damon, but strong and chaotic. Unfocused. Wordless. Without intention. But there.

I didn't have Greyson's willing body to keep me together, and I wasn't convinced that was a good thing. Damon hadn't wanted to hurt her, and I'd used his fear and distaste to frighten him away.

This new Thing wanted her pain like a thirsty man wanted water. Damon was gone, but I was still broken in two.

Disappointment became resentment. I walked away to suppress it. These guys didn't need to see me all wound up. But as I got to the edge of the roof, a hand locked painfully onto my bicep. It was Stoneface. I understood then where he'd gotten his name.

"We stay on this side of the stairs." He pointed at the concrete structure, then out at the tower where the voice was being projected from. "They have snipers in the minaret."

From there, they could have picked me off like a duck in a shooting range. Shoot out the star for a prize. I was less than human and more valuable for it.

I joined them in the circle of chairs.

On cue, after prayers ended, the bombs started in the distance. I remembered the sound of mortar fire all too well. So did the Thing I wouldn't call by name.

"Ah, shit." Agent Orange took his beer from his lips.

We peered out from behind the structure at the plumes of smoke.

"The Blackthorne guys were talking about a convoy out that way," Boner said.

Blackthorne. They were known for military contracting, not medical research. My blood chilled at the mention of the name anyway.

"Who's on the medevac?" Stoneface dropped his half-full beer back into the cooler.

"Catapult." Agent Orange looked at me. "The 61Js go out when the field surgeons are short."

"And they're always short," Heartland added. "Better get down there."

The Thing disappeared at the thought of going into the Red Zone, leaving nothing but fearless clarity. It wasn't afraid. It was satisfied.

Fucking Greyson hard was the way to get rid of Damon. This new Thing craved danger.

Chapter Five

GREYSON

Caden wasn't the only one with professional detachment. My work at the hospital went on as planned. When people asked about him, I told them he was deployed. I told them I was proud of him, and I was. He'd ripped himself apart to keep his promises. Who wouldn't have stood in awe over such a thing?

"I'll be in California Monday of next week," I told Leslie Yarrow. With a phone call and a credit card, I'd turned Damon's Hawaii trip into a flight to San Diego.

"I was going to mention this at the end," she said, rubbing her hands together as if she was nervous. "I've been stop-lossed."

"Oh." I was surprised. Troops seeking mental health care weren't usually sent back. "When are you leaving?"

"Tomorrow morning."

"Are you going to be all right?"

"Yeah. I really think I am. I have this. I feel like I can shut a lot of this off now."

She was the last patient of the day, and it was my second week without Caden. We'd had an unsatisfying call from Fort Bragg. He'd be in Iraq now.

I missed him.

The last months had been stressful. Damon's appearance had thrown me, and the months before that, with the unexpectedly rough sex and the more unexpected reason for it, had been a slow crawl of emotional tightness that unwound just as slowly without the day-to-day chaos.

In the unwinding, my own feelings were freed. Disappointment unraveled to reveal anxiety, which dissolved into a puddle of worry that boiled with anger that steamed into sadness before soaking into resentment.

With the coil of emotions unwound, I was left with a deconstruction of everything that overlaid the only thing that mattered.

Caden. Me. The love that bound us together wasn't connected to the skein I'd built around it. It stood discrete. It was at the heart of every decision I was about to make.

As an officer, Caden was allowed a cell phone, but the service was so spotty and he had it off so often I never got through.

When Yarrow told me she'd been stop-lossed despite her issues, I had to talk to him. His voice would take this spinning feeling and pin it down.

I started the calls in the afternoon. The AMEDD recruiter gave me his stateside unit contact, and from there, I knew enough of the right things to say to get me a number to the Baghdad CSH office. After midnight, when the sun was rising over Iraq's capitol, I sat at the edge of our bed and punched the numbers in the night table phone.

"He's off base," the nurse said after he'd looked at the chart.

"I'm sorry?"

"Probably be back in a few hours."

"Wait, Lieutenant, hold up," I said. "He's outside the wire?"

"Yes, ma'am."

"Is he in the Red Zone?"

"Everything outside the green is red, ma'am."

I had to stop myself from asking why he'd gone or if it was the first time. I thanked him and hung up.

HE SENT me an email with Skype names. Mine was MrsVitaminG. His was MajorRabbitsFoot.

I was sure any emotion that weakened him was still locked away, but I was glad that hadn't affected his sense of humor.

According to the email, the docs had chipped in to share an old computer and prohibitively expensive and totally crap Wi-Fi. I needed to dial in at two in the morning EST on Wednesday. The connection was terrible. It dropped three times before I heard him.

"Grey?" His voice came over the speaker.

The screen was black with a little red phone in the center and a slash through a video icon. I saw myself in the little rectangle on the lower left.

"I can't see you," I said.

"The camera on this thing doesn't work. I can see you. You look beautiful."

I patted an errant length of hair. I'd become a connoisseur of my husband's vocal inflections. He sounded like himself... mostly. Not like Damon, but not without a certain edge.

"You look like a little red camera with a slash through it."

"New uniforms."

I laughed. Sense of humor intact.

"How are you?" I asked. "I tried to call, and the nurse at the desk said you were off base?"

"It's different now. And Baghdad is different. We're in a permanent building. Not trailers."

He was changing the subject.

"Where did you go off base?"

"Not far."

I was embarrassed I'd asked the question. He wasn't allowed to give me any locations, and I was asking what any self-respecting army wife knew not to. "I'm just worried."

"You think I went to a brothel?"

"You wouldn't do that unless you wanted me to fly there and start burning shit down."

"You could put an end to the entire war."

"All you have to do is cheat on me."

"This war's going to go on a long time then."

"Yeah." I swallowed and tried not to think about it. "Have you heard from Damon?"

"No. Can you tuck your hair behind your ear? I want to see your throat."

My neck tingled from the attention. I pulled my hair

away, watching myself in the little box as I showed him the pale length of my throat. "Does it look okay?"

"I want to mark that neck so bad. I want to suck all the blood to the surface. Break the skin just a little with my teeth."

"You're alone, I hope?"

"Pull up your shirt."

Naively, I hadn't prepared mentally or physically for Skype sex, but there I was with wet panties anyway. I pulled the hem of my T-shirt up over my bra.

"Your tits, Grey." He sounded like a teacher I'd handed the wrong assignment. I pulled the sports bra over my breasts, showing my hard nipples to the little box that was my mirror and the black screen that was his window. "Yes. I want to mark those too."

"Where?"

"Underneath."

I ran my hand over my nipples to the soft skin underneath. "Here?"

"There. I'd bite you until you screamed."

I pinched a bit of skin and twisted it, cringing when it hurt, then pushing myself to twist harder.

"Grey,"—his blind whisper came over the speakers —"watch yourself do it."

Grunting, I watched as I bruised myself for him. It wasn't sexy, but it aroused me because it was for him.

He didn't speak until I whimpered.

"Stop," he said. "Show me."

I pulled my shirt and bra off in one motion and stood for the camera. The red mark was angry and raw. It wasn't finished either. It was going to blossom into a nasty bruise.

He sucked air through his teeth. The idea of him jerking off to my pain was arousing and sickening at the same time, with the arousal being fed by the aversion.

"Pants off. Everything off." I slid my pajama pants and underwear down, stepping out of them as he said, "Show me. Open your legs and show me."

My clit throbbed and grew heavy inside my seam as I angled the screen down so that when I sat with my feet on the desk and my legs spread, the little box in the corner centered around the space between my legs.

"I'm so turned on," I said, sliding my hand into my seam. "And I can't even see you."

"I can see you."

He said it as if his view was all that was important, and maybe he was right. I was there for him, and that satisfied me.

"I'd bite inside those thighs and make you stay still for it," he said with a rumbling depth. "I'd bring you to the edge and give you enough pain to pull you back, then start over until you begged for me to finish you."

All of that. I wanted all of it. Not just the orgasm I was about to give myself, but what he described. My fingers circled my clit in circles wide enough for him to see, but the movement brought me too close.

"You'd do it like this?" I tugged on a pinch of flesh inside my thigh, squeezing and twisting until it hurt, then doing it harder. My orgasm was a growling pit bull, held back by the leash of my pain.

"Leave a mark," he said, and I twisted into exquisite agony. The leash frayed but held.

"It hurts," I groaned as the pit bull bucked against her restraints.

"Like that. Come like that."

The orgasm broke free, and I went blind in a swirl of sensation, agony, and pleasure with every stage in between. Him watching my three-dimensional orgasm expanded it further, adding the conquest of humiliation and the embrace of shame.

Deaf inside my own experience, I didn't hear him come. I only heard his sigh at the end. I threw my head over the back of the chair and moved my hands away.

"Ow," I said.

"That's going to leave a bruise."

I bent as far as I could to see between my legs. "Yeah. No bikinis for me."

Slowly, I lowered my legs off the desk.

"I want to watch you get dressed," he said.

I pulled my shirt down, grimacing when I touched the spot I'd bruised under my breast.

"That's mine. Think of me when it hurts."

"Are you smiling?" I asked as I hopped back into my pants.

"A little."

"Do you have any more time?"

"Five minutes."

"What's it like? Your day? Just talk to me. I wonder what you're doing all the time."

"The surge isn't the same as Fallujah when we were there. Casualties are spread out. We haven't had anything like those eight days."

"I hear the Red Zone is constant guerilla warfare."

"Yeah. Less of a front line. More of a huge, very shitty neighborhood."

"And you're safe in the Green Zone?" I smoothed my clothes over my body.

"It's like a regular neighborhood, and I'm some asshole doing my job."

"When I called, they said you were outside the wire."

"It's different here, baby. You have nothing to worry about."

The bruise between my legs shot through with pain when I sat in the chair again. It would get worse before it got better, and that seemed exactly right.

"SURPRISE."

At nine thirty at night, two days after I'd bruised myself for Caden, Colin stood at my doorstep with a droll smile and a suitcase at his feet. My mother pushed past him with her arms out, and Dad came right behind her until I was crushed in a hug.

"What are you guys doing here?"

"Your mother—"

"I said I was coming with him or without him." Mom picked up her suitcase, but Dad shot Colin a look until his son took the hard-sided case.

I got out of the way and let the three of them in. "It's a bit of a mess. I can't believe you came."

"You sounded so sad," Mom said. "I couldn't wait until you came to us."

"This is quite a place," Dad said, letting himself into the living room. He was checking out the furniture and woodwork.

"Priceless, apparently," I said. "I haven't set up the guest rooms, but—"

"We can get a hotel," Mom said.

"No, no—"

"It's all right," Dad chimed in. "The city's full of them."

"They haven't seen the prices," Colin said.

"Yeah." I picked up the suitcase. "You're staying here. This house is huge, and honestly, it's wasted."

My parents jumped at the opportunity to reduce waste.

AFTER A TRIP to the linen closet for sheets and towels, I settled them into the guest bedroom. With military efficiency, we made the bed and got the clothes in the drawers. My father closed the closet with a definitive *click*, and I took a deep breath.

"I'm so glad you came," I said.

"We're always there for you," he replied.

"I just... I thought I had this, but now that you're here, it's like I didn't realize how much I wanted to be near people who understand."

"That was the thing your mother always had on base. A community. You don't have that luxury in the shitstorm city like this."

I'd always considered that community oppressive, but I'd only seen it from the point of view of a disaffected teenager.

"She woulda died of loneliness without those magpies," Dad continued as we walked downstairs. "But everywhere we went, there was a group of women who didn't look at her funny or exclude her."

"What are you telling her?" Mom had made herself right at home in my kitchen. The teapot was warming, and she'd cut cheese slices I'd left in the fridge into bite-sized pieces. They were fanned out along the edges of a plate, a stack of crackers in the center. Little bowls of olives and pickles were set out on the island.

Colin was tapping on his Blackberry.

"I'm telling her you weren't miserable." Dad slid onto a stool and popped an olive in his mouth. "You might wanna back me up."

She shook her head. "I don't wish that life on you," she said to me. "But it could've been worse. Cracker?"

Nothing like being offered your own food in your own house. I took a cracker and put a piece of cheese on it.

"Have you spoken to him?" Mom asked.

"We had a Skype call."

"How is he?"

"Fine."

"Why the fuck did he go in again?" Colin got right to the point once he'd put his Blackberry down. "I thought he was done."

"He was." I pressed my fingers to the counter to get the crumbs up.

"So, what was he thinking?"

"Colin!" Dad scolded. "Just because you don't understand a sense of duty doesn't mean it doesn't exist."

My brother rolled his eyes. My father wagged his finger twice. This was such an old argument between them that they could get into it and out of it without actually having it.

"What are you guys going to do while you're here?" I asked. "You going full tourist or just hanging out?"

"Whatever's easy for you—"

"No," Colin interrupted. "Why, Grey? You won't answer me when I ask you, so maybe you'll answer in front of Mom and Dad. Why did he sign on again?"

Our parents would try to deflect, but the question would remain. In Colin, the family tenacity had manifested in curiosity. I'd have to address it at some point.

"He did it for me," I said, glancing at my mother, who was frozen with a pickle halfway to her mouth. "I wanted him to take part in something, and he had to be in the reserves to do it."

"Something?" Colin raised an eyebrow.

He knew about Day Caden and Night Caden. Was he being intentionally thick, or was I being too cryptic?

"I told you he had PTSD, Colin."

"Ah!" Everything must have clicked for him because he picked up his Blackberry again.

Dad held up his hand. "Wait, wait, wait."

"He's fine," I said. "He had to be in the reserve system for the treatment, and he got called. End of story."

As if to punctuate my reluctance to speak further on it, the teapot whistled.

"Well," Mom said, turning down the heat, "he's a good man. I worried about you with men."

"Mom. I'm deeply offended. I didn't have a ton of boyfriends."

"Two words," Colin said. "Scott Verehoven."

"Hey!" Dad snapped. "We don't mention that name."

"What? Why?"

All three of them started talking at once. Colin called for Jesus Christ. Dad cursed. Mom *tsk*ed.

"That boy." Mom shook her head, pouring tea for Dad.

"Douchebag," Colin mumbled. My brother had been at UCLA the same time as me, though he hadn't been in ROTC.

I shrugged. "Everyone dates a douchebag at some point."

"When he called you a dyke in front of your entire patrol," Colin said, "and all his friends thought it was hilarious?"

"There's nothing wrong with being gay," I said, taking my teacup. I'd gotten a haircut, and yeah, there was nothing wrong with being gay, but he'd meant it as an insult, and it had hurt my feelings. He was supposed to be my boyfriend.

"And the diving board." Colin went to pick up his Blackberry again but just flicked it across the counter. "Asshole."

"Platform," I said. "It was the platform."

LOS ANGELES

MAY 1994

THE NIGHT SCOTT called me a dyke was my twentieth birthday. My patrol had told him to shut the fuck up. Even Nancy, who was indeed a lesbian, told him to go pound sand up his ass or she'd do it herself. He left in a huff.

At midnight, I slipped away to find him. The gate to the high dive was open. He was a star and had the key so he could start practice at four thirty in the morning. His body landed in the water like a knife, a dark blade against a darker backdrop.

"Hey," I said from the edge of the pool as he surfaced. "Sorry about Nancy."

I shouldn't have apologized for my friend. She was wonderful. He was an asshole. But I was newly twenty and continually insecure.

"She knows I can't do anything to her." He bowed his back and went underwater. The muscles of his back were molded in the moonlight, shaped like the surface of the water.

We'd only made out and done some groping in the six weeks we'd been dating. He acted as if he'd put all this work into grooming me and gotten nothing in return. I should have dumped him. He was beautiful to look at, but he never made an attempt to be a nice person. I stayed with him because I liked the way other girls looked at me when we were together. The ROTC uniform made me look like a dumpy asexual. Having those sexed, free, powerful young women look at me as if I could be one of them made me feel sexed, free, and powerful too.

Scott got out of the water. Compared to most of the country, Los Angeles nights were warm in May, but his nipples were hard and his pecs were pulled into tight mounds.

"You coming in?" he asked, taking stock of my body in modest civilian clothes.

"I can't dive." I couldn't swim well either. And I wasn't great with heights.

He shrugged and headed for the ladder, his shoulder blades sharp wedges under his skin, wet shorts falling just below his waist to reveal a perfectly formed Adonis belt.

Beauty aside, he'd challenged me by climbing up that ladder. I kicked off my shoes and stuffed my socks in them. I didn't have to dive if I didn't want to, right? I peeled off my jeans, folded them, and put them on a chair with my jacket.

"Come on then." He was past the lower platform already.

In my underwear and T-shirt, I went up the ladder.

"I REMEMBER the look on his father's face," Dad said in my kitchen fourteen years later, smiling with the inner satisfaction that comes from reliving a great memory.

"When?" I asked.

He and Mom exchanged a glance.

Scott's father had blamed me for the fall, complaining to the dean that since I wasn't on the diving team, I had no business by the pool at all.

Dad shrugged. "You got any sugar for this tea?"

"It's right in front of you. When did you meet Scott's father?"

Mom tapped her foot. "Might as well tell her."

"Yeah, Dad," Colin said.

"Well." He stirred sugar into his tea. "Jakey and I met up with him on this little street in Palisades and had a talk with him."

"A talk?"

Colin chuckled.

"These pussy Hollywood types spook easy." He waved off the gravity of whatever it was he'd done. "They see a rifle and start praying."

"What?"

"We just talked, Grey." Colin waved it off.

"You were there? You were barely eighteen!"

"I had a driver's license."

Dad laughed. "He drove him off the road. Scared the hell out of us."

"What?"

"I stayed in the car," Colin protested from behind his cup. "I didn't get to put a rifle butt through his windows."

I couldn't believe what I was hearing. It was so outrageous I couldn't speak.

Dad took that as permission to find humor in the story. "He was shaking so hard I thought he was going to create his own weather pattern."

"What did you say to him?" I was stunned. I couldn't imagine that ending well.

"Not a word. Jake just kept grunting at him. He's a funny kid. Laughed the whole way home."

Colin—my refined, intelligent brother—smirked at the violence. "They just broke his windows and his cell phone. Words would have been superfluous."

"Jesus Christ, guys."

"He'd come a long way from going to the hospital with a rifle." Mom sipped her tea.

"You knew about this?"

"Of course. Can you eat the cheese you took, please?"

I picked up my cheese but stopped it on the way to my mouth. "I don't know whether to yell at you guys or thank you."

"Don't thank me," Dad said. "You thanked me by graduating and getting a commission. If you want to yell, you're a grown woman. You can yell if you want."

I ate the cheese and chewed pensively, realizing I wished I had been there to smash Mr. Verehoven's windows with an assault weapon just to see his fear create a weather pattern.

I'D NEVER TOLD my dad I was afraid of falling. He was in the 101st. It was his job to jump out of planes. I didn't want him to be disappointed in me. After hearing about the broken car windows, I was even more glad. Who knew what he would have done if he'd had any idea how terrified I was of falling from a height?

With Colin gone and my parents tucked in, I couldn't sleep. The memory of getting pushed off that ten-meter diving platform haunted me. I had been convinced I was going to die, and inside the conviction had been a clarity that expanded time. From the high platform, a diver spends about 1.42 seconds going straight down.

The water had had a misleading gentle turquoise glow from the underwater lights. The surface—I knew—would hit my body with the force of concrete if I landed flat.

My neck would break.

Near-death lucidity was a very real phenomena. It expanded time and mental capabilities. It allowed me to hold my breath. It gave me time to turn just enough to tuck my arms to my body and protect my neck so I only devastated my shoulder.

I lived a full life in a second and a half.

My terror of heights didn't come from the injuries. It came from the second and a half of clarity. Feeling, seeing, hearing everything. Elongating the string of time into an elastic band the exact length of the rest of my life.

Near-death lucidity was my limit. A hard no.

When Scott had half apologized at my hospital bedside, admitting to no more than clumsiness, I thought he'd had a change of heart. I hadn't realized my family had gone full military.

Not that it would have mattered. I'd told Scott to go fuck himself. I hadn't trusted myself with men for a long time after that. I dated on my terms and had sex on my terms.

The night Dad had admitted he'd "facilitated" the diver's exit from UCLA, I stared at the ceiling with my arms folded over my chest, listening to the soft, irregular hum of traffic and trying to feel remorse or guilt. I had none. Scott could still go fuck himself.

I'd kept myself in complete control until Caden.

I'd chosen wisely. He was worth my trust.

Chapter Six

CADEN

The first time I'd gone outside the wire, in Fallujah, it had been a mess. I didn't talk about it. Ever. I hadn't even told Greyson anything more than "Everyone lived, no problems." After filling out the report, I'd shoved the incident into the back of my mind, where it died a quiet death so that I could live.

My first trip out in Baghdad shut down the Thing before the Blackhawk even got off the ground. We circled over a patch of road with the median blasted out. The injured was lifted onto deck, and I treated him. We went back to the Green Zone without touching the ground.

The Thing came back as soon as I got off the helicopter.

Was it the idea of danger that ran it off the road? How shitty did it have to get before it gave me some space?

I'd had a call with my wife that night. She'd done to herself what I needed to do to her, and it was fucking amazing. The Thing was gone. That space in my mind was filled with Greyson, and it was strong.

COL. DELEON—NO one called her Harpy or even Karen to her face—threw herself into the chair next to me. There were two adjacent desks in the tiny office, each with a beige computer we all used for notes, reports, and requisitions.

"How you holding up, Asshole Eyes?"

That, apparently, was my nickname. My father had been an asshole, they were his eyes, and bang—nickname. Could have been worse. She'd called me Pretty Boy once, and I'd given her a look that made the buzz in my ears even louder. She knew enough about leadership to back off. I appreciated that.

Not looking away from the computer I typed notes into, I answered, "Good."

She tapped her password into the other machine. "Heard you were at Balad for the first few days of Phantom Fury."

"Yeah."

"Eight days straight."

"More like seven and three quarters."

"Impressive."

"Not a big deal."

"You speak Arabic too?"

"I understand enough. My wife speaks it."

Mentioning Greyson was completely unnecessary yet critical.

We worked for a few minutes, then she twisted her chair to face me and crossed her legs. "Why'd you resign your commission?"

"Personal reasons."

"It seemed strange," she said, blowing right by my answer, "because you're really good at this. You belong here."

Finished, I logged out and turned to her. "I'll take that as a compliment."

"It is."

"Thank you."

"You don't like me much, do you?"

"Are you here to be liked?"

"Hell no." She smiled and crossed her arms to match her legs. "It's not about you learning about me. It's about me learning about you. A lot of guys take issue working under a woman, and I need to know where you stand on that."

"I'm fine with it."

"I know. You all are. But some of you have a little voice inside you that's bothered by it, and it's my job"—her voice got very feminine and seductive—"to tease out that tiny voice, little by little, so I can *crush* it." She said "crush" with a growl and a clenched fist.

I laughed. I couldn't help it, and neither could she.

"My little voice has been crushed," I said, holding up my hands. "Trust me."

Her eyes fell on my wedding ring, then on my asshole eyes.

WOMEN FLIRTED WITH ME. I knew it when I saw it, but I wasn't particularly good at it. When I made an innuendo or expressed a desire, it was because I planned to follow through. Promising sex without the intention of delivering it was a waste of everyone's time.

I was sure I hadn't given DeLeon reason to believe I was interested in flirting or fucking. She'd seen my ring. I'd seen the fact that she didn't have one. Not that it mattered. Married people fucked around all the time. Just not me.

But I had a problem. I was back to square one with a new Thing. It was in the sounds and the shadows. In the midnight chanting from the minaret and the muffled voices behind doors, it buzzed. It wasn't frightened away; it was satisfied away, like a noisy cat being scratched behind the ear. It was quieted by danger, surgery, and Greyson's pain.

Danger came when it did, and surgery was regular but unplannable. Without Greyson's body, I didn't know how to stifle the presence. Without access to her pain, I couldn't placate it.

"Eyes!" Heartland ran up behind me as I checked the charts. He refused the word "asshole" like a vegetarian refused meat. "Nine-line. Boner's in OR."

"I'll go."

AS THE BLACKHAWK LIFTED UPWARD, inertia tried to pull my stomach downward. I usually took this as a sign of my discomfort in the air, but with the reappearance of the Thing came the slippery shaft I pushed my emotions into. Fear went right into the locked box.

We arrived over a rocky dry riverbed in four minutes.

"Aw, shit," the pilot said in my headset.

I looked down, something I would have struggled to do without my personal emotional sponge, and took in the scene.

An overturned truck. Two stopped but upright. A plume of smoke. A perimeter of men on their stomachs protecting the center. A man waving a sign for sniper fire. Two men crouched over another lying on his back. The pool of blood enclosed him in a huge, black comma.

They weren't military.

"We can't land under fire," the copilot, Gangrene, said in my headset.

"That's a lot of blood," I replied.

"Fucking contractors," the paramedic grumbled.

"He's going to die," I said, turning to make eye contact with the medics, then the pilot and copilot.

"Fuck!" the pilot barked. "Are we in or not?"

"I'm in." If the doc answered first, it was easier for the other guys to agree, and I knew they wanted to.

They chimed in their agreement, the contractor-hating paramedic consenting last.

The Blackhawk whipped around and swooped down.

Trapped in a speeding tin can, hurtling into sniper fire with the angry Thing boiled into adrenaline, I'd never felt so free.

Chapter Seven

GREYSON

It was eight thirty in the morning in Baghdad when I called. Army lunchtime.

"Corporal Lorben. How can I help you?"

"I'm looking for Dr. St. John. This is his wife."

"He's not here. Do you want to leave a message?"

No, I did not want to leave a message. I wanted to hear my husband's voice.

"When is he on duty?" I asked.

"I think he's on his way back from a medevac."

What?

"No, that's..."

Not possible.

Not right.

Not allowed.

Stop acting surprised.

My hope that his last trip out had been a one-time deal got shot out of the sky.

"Ma'am?"

"Let him know I called. It's not an emergency."

IF SLEEP WASN'T HAPPENING, I could at least go to my office and get work done. On the way down, I heard my father making his "night noises." Huffs of fear. Startled jumps. As I passed, he made the *uh-uh-uh* that could go on for minutes.

The PTSD never left him, but he'd never admitted he had it. Mom had stopped nagging him years ago.

Don't let Caden become like Dad.

I hurried downstairs, banishing the thought. Keeping busy was the trick. I packed up the files of the patients I'd referred out and the ones moving to the hospital practice.

Decisions are made before they're made. The seeds are planted and watered, growing invisibly under the surface until the sprouts show, and even then, with those first two spear-shaped leaves, we can't identify the fruit they'll bear.

But a seed had been planted. I just couldn't see it in the noise of daily life. I had bills to pay, a business to wind down, a dream job to ramp up, and patients who needed care.

As I went through the files, I noticed where they'd come from. Some of my first military clients had come from Jenn, but even more had come from Ronin.

I'd stacked the files in order of where they were going, but I restacked them according to where they'd come from, then I looked at the names.

I knew them. I knew their problems, their struggles, and the details of their PTSD.

I wrote down the names of those who had described feelings of dissociation. Most were mild and had shown improvement. One had gotten worse, but he'd been stop-lossed two weeks before and I couldn't check on him.

Weird.

They weren't supposed to stop-loss troops with PTSD. Maybe Caden hadn't been an exception.

But in a way, Caden was part of a larger pattern.

All of the dissociative cases had come from Ronin.

———

"COINCIDENCE," Ronin said casually. His body was turned to the side, and his legs were stretched out while his elbow rested on the table as if he wanted to be fully present but also needed to be able to leave the coffee shop quickly.

"Were any of them getting the same treatment as Caden?"

"You know I can't tell you that."

"How did you expect me to help these people if they weren't forthcoming about what other treatments they were receiving?"

"Nothing you prescribed interfered with what we were doing." He was such a baldly self-involved ass that I didn't have an immediate reply, which gave him room to wedge in more excuses. "Overall, did your PTSD patients have a normal ratio of disorders or not?"

"The problem is that they all came from you."

He shrugged. "Your sample is too small to determine that I'm the problem here." He turned his body around to face me fully. "What we're doing is important work, and it's safe work. It's for us. For the country and for the life of every soldier in the field."

"You going to vomit stars and stripes now?"

"You're looking for a reason your husband broke. The fact is there is no reason. It just is. Some people break, some crack, some are fine. Look at you." He put his hand out as if presenting me on a silver platter. "You're fine."

Was I fine? Maybe. I slept. I ate. I loved.

After the carnival where I'd stared down a fear of mortar fire, I didn't jump at whistles or booms. My mind had snapped back like a new rubber band. I hadn't identified any triggers that changed my mood or caused a sharp negative reaction.

So, I was fine. I was the end of a long line of soldiers.

I had been born for this.

"I want you to send me back," I said.

"Excuse me?"

"Blackthorne's contracting security in Iraq. I want to go back. Hire me."

"Wait, wait, wait..." He shook his head.

"A psych on staff can reduce your liability when your teams come back with PTSD."

"We have no liability."

I wasn't ready to blame Ronin or Blackthorne for my husband's condition. It had started before the treatment, and it had gotten better under it. But he'd been sent away because of them and they owed me. "Hire me."

"It doesn't work like that."

"Tell me how it works and make it happen."

"Why don't you just sign on for another commission?"

"Because they'll put me where they want me. I could end up in Korea. Blackthorne will put me near my husband."

"I always thought you were crazy." He stood and placed his hands flat on the table so he could lean close to me. "You're still gorgeous, but you're still out of your goddamn mind."

"I'll get on a plane to Jordan right now and walk to Baghdad. If I have to do that, Ronin, if I have to go as a free agent, I'm talking to every left-wing, contractor-hating journalist who'll listen."

"About what exactly?"

"All I have to do is make them curious about what you're doing here. They already hate you because of Abu Ghraib. Hire me, station me where I want to go, and you'll have your NDA."

He stood straight and buttoned his jacket. "It's been great catching up."

"CADEN?"

"I heard you called?"

It was one in the morning, and as soon as the phone rang, I knew it was him.

"Are you all right?" I asked.

"I'm fine. Everything's fine."

Sure. Everything was fine. This whole thing was over, and we could go on like a normal couple.

"How's Damon?"

He breathed into the receiver, cleared his throat. I waited. The sound of people talking in the background was cut off after the click of a door and the squeak of a desk chair.

"I'm managing it," Caden answered finally.

"How?"

"I want to get you on Skype. I need to see your cunt."

Blood flowed between my legs with an urgency that ached. "My parents are here. In the house."

"I don't care."

"I want to talk about the medevac."

"Do everything I say and tell me you're doing it." His resolve left no room for my concern. It flooded me with a desire to please him. "Take off your clothes."

After dropping the phone on the bed, I wriggled out of my shirt and underpants and put the phone to my ear again. "I'm naked."

"God, Grey. Just thinking about you... I want to tear you apart. I want to stretch you open until you scream. I want to take your air away. Hold you down by the throat until your cunt tightens around me. Watch your face when you wake up coming."

"Do it."

"Get on your knees. On the floor."

In the half a second it took me to feel the bite of the wood surface on my hard knees, I reclaimed a corner of my mind. With the cordless phone on the floor between my hands, I bent over it in humiliating supplication, still refusing to give up. "Why were you on a medevac again?"

The resolve in my voice might not have matched his for control and confidence, but my insistence wasn't in question.

"The rules changed. Put your hand between your legs."

"What rules?"

"Are you wet?"

I didn't need to touch myself to know I was open and dripping for him, but I did anyway. "Yes."

"They're short 62Bs. I can go over the wire."

"You can, or you have to?"

"The bruise inside your thigh. Touch it."

The bruise from the previous week had faded to yellow, but touching it reminded me of the pain. I audibly sucked air at the thought.

"That's mine," he said. "I think about it when I'm on the Blackhawk. Your pain keeps me focused."

"I think of you when it hurts."

"Touch your clit for me."

I did as he asked, running two fingers along my hard nub, deep into myself, and back to my clit, groaning with pleasure.

"Did you volunteer for the medevac?"

"It's me or someone else. I want to taste you. Put my lips on you. Suck it between my teeth so hard you don't know whether you're screaming in pain or pleasure."

"I'm going to come," I said almost sadly. The bite of loneliness clamped around the edge of my orgasm, holding it still in the chambers of my heart. "God, just tell me what's going on there."

I needed him. I needed his touch, his kiss, his voice, his life in mine.

"I don't mind being here," he said. "But without you, it's hell. Anywhere in the world you're not is hell for me."

"I'm coming," I said, and the present and future wound together in the same sentence. "I'm coming. I'm coming. I'm coming."

WHEN HE'D SAID his life was hell without me, he'd had no idea he was stamping and sealing an engraved invitation. The fact was the invitation had been printed the minute I found out he was over the wire for the second time.

Or third. Or tenth. I had no idea how often he went. My ignorance gnawed at my confidence.

"I'm not exactly walking across Jordan." I whipped a pair of thick cargo pants out of the drawer. "That was just a manner of speaking."

Dad sat in the bedroom chair. "You have no idea what you're doing."

"No one does until they do it."

"I mean those clothes. It's in the eighties in Baghdad. You want to sweat your skin off?"

"Oh, right." I pulled a pile of underpants out of my drawer and threw them on the bed. "I'll wear my gym shorts and a rib tank. Should I bother with a bra?"

"You were always a wiseass."

"It's a defense mechanism." I rolled up the pants and tucked them into a corner of my duffel bag.

"Defends you from listening to common sense."

"I'm uncommon." From my dresser, I picked up a small photo in a silver frame. Caden and I in our wedding gear. Tux and white gown, on the beach in San Diego. Faces full of sand. We'd stopped in the middle of the photo shoot to build a sand castle. "I make uncommon decisions and do uncommon things."

"Like show up in the Green Zone to see your husband."

"I'm devoted." I put the picture back. Baghdad wasn't the place for sand castles and wedding gowns. "What can I say?" The front doorbell rang. I leaned out into the hall and called down the stairs, "Ma? Can you get that?"

"All right!"

Dad continued as if uninterrupted. "How do you think he's going to react to you going there?"

My mouth tightened into a wry smile, and I shrugged, picking up a hoodie and rolling it into a log. "He's going to be pissed."

"Why's that make you smile?"

"I don't know." I jammed the hoodie in the bag and reached into my underwear drawer. "Maybe because if I was a boy and I traveled over the surface of the earth for a woman, you'd give me the same advice but you'd be proud I took some initiative."

"That is not true."

"It is true. I love you, but you never understood me. I never acted the way you thought a girl should."

"No, I mean, I am proud of you. I can be proud of the decisions you want to make and think they're stupid at the same time. You want him back? You have access to all the channels you need right here. You tell them he's got PTSD, and they'll put him on a plane so fast it'll give you whiplash."

"And the divorce will come right after."

"Better divorced than dead."

"Yeah... no." I zipped the bag. "You have those in the wrong order."

"Greyson?" Mom stood in the bedroom doorway and handed me a manila envelope.

There was no address. Just my name printed onto a sticky white label and a red stamp. CONFIDENTIAL. Once I took it, she started wringing her hands.

"They still deliver death notices personally, Ma." I tore open the envelope.

"I know, I know."

The cover letter slid off before I could read it, revealing the first page of a contract.

NONDISCLOSURE AGREEMENT between

BLACKTHORNE SOLUTIONS INCORPORATED (the Company)

And

DR. GREYSON FRAZIER (*the Independent Contractor*)

"YES!" I threw my arms in the air, but my parents didn't share my enthusiasm.

MY FAMILY WORKED hard to talk me out of it, but they'd tried to talk me out of everything I'd ever wanted. Military service (too restrictive for my personality). Med school (too expensive). Voluntary deployment (too dangerous). Everything except marrying Caden. I'd stopped holding their objections against them long ago. They loved me, and they'd always tried to talk me out of things that made them proud.

Everything would be fine. The thought of taking this problem into my hands outweighed their opposition by a few metric tons.

I had work to do, and that made me happy.

THE GRAY DOT by MajorRabbitsFoot turned green, and the red camera with the slash through it disappeared. I thought the thing was broken and I was going to have to reconnect. But it wasn't.

His face.

He took my breath away.

I think I gasped. I was sure a high-pitched sound escaped my lips. I covered my mouth.

I must have looked shocked or displeased, because he ran his fingers through his hair, and I took mine off my mouth to touch the screen. It prickled with electricity, smooth and cool to the touch. Nothing like him. He was rough and warm. If I could have run my hands over the T-shirt that clung to him, his skin and muscles would have yielded only so much, and the dog tags that dangled over his chest would have clinked softly when they moved.

"Are you all right?" The sound was a split second behind the movement of his lips.

"I forgot."

"Forgot what? Are you sick? What happened?"

When I got close to the screen, he broke into tiny points of light. His skin color was pale yellow from the monitor. He'd lost weight. I preferred a little scruff on his cheeks to the clean-shaven, boyish look. His hair was too short, and the webcam stole the sky from his eyes.

"I forgot what you looked like."

I must have been clenching my fist the entire time he was away. Muscles I'd learned about in anatomy, but never used, uncoiled and melted into warm relief.

The morning I'd woken up from the nightmare that I was marrying the wrong man, I'd felt the same release. Everything would be all right as long as Caden was with me. The relief didn't come from my lungs or from my heart, but from cell and tissue. This was the man. He was mine. He was imprinted onto my neurons, triggering a hum and flash in my brain when the planes and angles of his face appeared.

He was beautiful. His smile was the answer to questions I hadn't even thought to ask. And the response was always yes.

I was more sure than ever that I was doing the right thing, and in that whirl of optimism, I forgot that we were separate people. I let go of all my plans to tell gentle half-truths or guide him through my maze of intentions.

"I'm coming!" I shouted, imagining his skin under my fingers. His voice, his scent, his presence with mine. I could barely contain myself. "I'm coming."

He blinked, tilted his head a little. The muscles around his left eye tightened. "I didn't even start."

I laughed. The English language had really fucked it up

by making homonyms of an orgasm and an arrival. "I'm coming to Baghdad!"

"You're... when? For how long?" I knew he was calculating how long he'd need to get an R&R request in. I was about to free him from that, but he got more words in first. "You just started the new job. It's not going to look good if you take a vacation right away."

"It's not a vacation. It's—"

"I'm really confused here, Grey."

"I got another job. With Blackthorne. I'm heading out to you."

I should have expected that to go poorly, but the sight of his face had sent me over the side of the road.

"I'm sorry." He tried to make some kind of sense out of what I'd said. "You lost me."

"I'm working on a deal with Mt. Sinai. It was really the plan they wanted; anyone can implement it. I—"

"Anyone can implement it?"

"It's connect-the-dots. I'm not special."

"Like fuck you aren't!"

I rubbed the sweat from my palms. All my arousal and excitement curdled into sour clusters.

"What are you thinking?" he asked. "What's going on in your mind?"

I miss you.

Those three words took up the bottom line.

I was worried about him. I wanted to check on him. I was the only one he trusted, and I needed to be there if something went wrong with the dissociation, but the last words on the matter were longing and desire.

I missed him.

"It's going to be all right," I said. "I'm not providing security. Just tending to the mental health of the contractors."

"Let me get this straight." He leaned on his elbows, getting his beautiful face closer to the camera. Since my camera was on top of my screen, he couldn't see when I touched the bottom of it to caress his glass chin. "Ronin hired you as a private contractor because Blackthorne gives a shit about the mental health of their security guys?"

"It's single site inside the Green Zone."

"You expect me to believe he came to you with this and you left a job you've been working to get for months to take it?"

"Yes."

"No." He leaned back, and his body slid away until my fingers touched the glass of his stomach. "No, no, no."

"You think I'm lying?" Typical defense mechanism.

Assume the worst. Force them to say no. Say they're sorry. Backpedal just a little.

"Yes. I do." Caden didn't take the bait. I hadn't married him because he was easily manipulated.

"Great. Thanks."

"First, you're lying to yourself."

"I wish I'd never sent you that webcam."

"Dane's wife sent one first. Yours hasn't gotten here yet. And that's another lie."

"You don't want me to come."

"No fucking shit, baby."

"You don't think I can handle myself?"

He slapped his hands on the table. "Why is everything a fucking pissing match with you?"

Don't cry, Major Frazier. "What—?"

"You can handle yourself, okay? If there's a person in the world who can handle herself, it's you. But admit it to me, your husband, that you want to be here because you never wanted to leave the army in the first place."

Don't you fucking cry. "That's not why."

"But it's true."

"It's true, but it's not why."

"So, you sold your soul to a company of douchebags to pretend you're a soldier again."

"Fuck you," I whispered.

"No, fuck you. Admit it."

"You're wrong."

"Admit you sold your soul to a mercenary organization—"

"No."

"With zero accountability."

"Wrong." My denial was barely a breath. It was a river in Egypt.

"Admit it."

Slapping my hands on the desk, I shouted, "I sold my soul to *you*, you fucking asshole!"

He fell back, slouching and staring past the camera into some middle distance inside himself.

What did he see there?

Guilt. He harbored it for things he hadn't done and fed it meals of things he'd never intended.

"Caden."

"Yeah, I... I don't know what to do."

"There's nothing to do. I'm coming. I sold my soul to you because I love you. I need you. I can't live without you."

He rubbed his forehead and looked toward the window. The light washed out his features. "It's not safe here."

"I know."

"The contractors. They're not protected. Not accountable and not protected."

"It's going to be fine."

"When they die, there's no official count. Blackthorne doesn't release numbers."

"Caden, it'll be all right. I'm not going out on security details. I'm just in some kind of office. They got me a house with a gate to live in."

He huffed a derisive laugh, as if his wire trumped my gate. "I shouldn't have done this," he said more to himself than me. "I should have just learned to live with it."

He was talking about the experimental *soo-hoo*s and the shots I was becoming more and more suspicious of.

"Are you living with it now?"

The question was rhetorical. I expected him to say no. Then I'd tell him it was worth it. He'd be mollified. I'd be soothed. We could continue normally. Maybe have a little fake sex.

But he didn't say no.

"Yeah," he said into the light from the window before looking back at the camera. "It's like it was. I can feel something's off, but I know what it is now. It's manageable."

Manageable?

Human beings were capable of selecting memories to suit their attitudes about present circumstances. We forgot the pain of childbirth to have more babies. We leaned over the toilet, swearing we'd never drink again, then said thank you when offered a fresh glass of wine.

"You almost killed me," I said, trying to state a fact rather than make an accusation. "You were in a constantly paranoid state that was pretty justified."

"I was managing. It's not worth this mess."

"We're going to be together. That's not a mess."

"It's a mess, Greyson. We're a mess."

I jolted, gulping breath, trying to think through the over-firing synapses. By defining our marriage as an unacceptable result instead of a difficult evolution, he'd broken through a limit I hadn't known I had. "Don't say that."

"I'm sorry. You don't have to like it, but it's the truth. We had something great, and we fucked it up."

"No," I growled through clenched teeth. "We still have something great. We're not past tense. We are a now. We are a future. We're happiness and hope, goddammit, and I won't let you talk like this."

The lips I'd been so happy to see pressed into a tight line. They lost their fullness, their generosity consumed in doubt. "I love you, Greyson."

"I know you do."

"This isn't about loving you."

"I know that too. But you're still wrong."

"I want you to stay home."

"This isn't about what you want either. I'll see you soon."

On the other side of the world, there was a knock at the door.

"I have to go," he said.

"Okay."

"Don't come. I mean it."

"I know you do."

The door behind him cracked open, and a bald white guy peered. He smiled at me, and when Caden turned to him, he jerked his head as if to tell my husband his presence was required.

We said our good-byes and cut the connection. The red camera with the line through it appeared again.

Nothing Caden had said had dissuaded me. I was more determined than ever to be with him.

Some forms of madness felt more lucid than sanity.

Chapter Eight

CADEN

Boner came all the way in when I hung up. "Sorry, man. My mom's waiting. You weren't jerking off or anything?"

"No." I stood so he could see my dick in my pants.

"You all right? You're white as an Irish ass." He sat in the chair and logged on.

"I'll get some sun."

"I have beer in my room if you need one."

"Thanks. I have to be in recovery." I started out just as his mother came onscreen.

"You're late, Matty."

I left, taking my worry with me.

THE CONTRACTOR we'd picked out of a giant comma of blood was in the ICU. Walter Benedict's chart put him at thirty-three, from Tucson. He'd needed two gallons of blood to replace what had been lost from his femoral artery. Agent Orange had managed to save his leg and his life. He was good, that guy.

"How are you doing?" I asked him.

"Feel like shit, sir." He didn't have to call me sir, but the fact that he did told me a lot.

"You lost a lot of blood." I sat by his bed. "Your body's busy making more."

"They're going to send me home, do you think?" His eyes were red-rimmed over dark circles. If he had been military, he'd have gone to Germany, then home, but he wasn't military.

"I have no idea how it works for you guys, but you made it. That's a good thing."

"Sure."

"What was your rank when you were enlisted?"

"Made it to staff sergeant. But the money... shit."

Contractors were well paid. He probably made twice as much running security details as he had when he was a soldier. Since Blackthorne was a private company, they could provide as much medical care to the wounded as they wanted. The VA was inadequate, but Blackthorne, again, could do what they wanted, be it too much or too little.

"You'll be on your feet in no time."

"Thanks, doc. For coming to get me. You didn't have to land under fire."

"Thank the pilot."

"Sure, sure." His eyes fluttered half-closed.

"Get some rest."

He obeyed almost instantly.

I didn't want my wife here. Not as a soldier. Especially not as a Blackthorne contractor. I did the rest of the rounds with my job on the perimeter of my mind and Greyson at the center.

She wouldn't be talked out of it. I hadn't married a pliable woman. The very things I loved about her were the things that made her difficult to keep.

She wouldn't come if she wasn't allowed, but I had no power over that.

She wouldn't come if I convinced her it would make the situation worse.

Or if she was needed at home.

Or if I wasn't here.

Bells rang in the back of my mind.

She won't come if I'm not here.

WHEN I KNOCKED GENTLY on Colonel DeLeon's door, the buzz of the Thing got lower and denser, as if it knew I was trying to get out of harm's way. Its presence had increased steadily since my last medevac, growing into an infuriating distraction. I needed to make it to my next Skype with Greyson. A long-distance pain play would put the Thing away, sleeping like a guest crashing on the couch after Thanksgiving dinner.

DeLeon's office was tiny with gray plaster walls, metal filing cabinets, and a window with white paint on the glass. She had her elbow on the desk and her fingers threaded in her hair as she hunched over paperwork.

"Yeah?" She didn't look up.

"I need to talk to you."

"Close the door." She sat back and indicated the black office chair in front of the desk. The upholstery was ripped on the right armrest and the edge of the seat.

I took off my hat and sat.

"What can I do for you, Dr. St. John?"

"No Asshole Eyes?"

"You look too serious for fucking around right now."

"I appreciate that."

"Good."

I didn't want to ask her—or anyone—for anything when I had no leverage.

When I'd taken too long to speak, she said, "I don't bite."

"I need leave." I didn't sound like I'd blurted it out, but I had.

Leaning forward on the desk, she folded her hands in front of her. "Why?"

"It's personal."

"Yeah. I know. But I get to ask. That's how it works."

She did, and I knew I'd have to answer.

"My wife signed on with Blackthorne."

DeLeon stayed stock-still except for two fingers she tapped together twice, then arched an eyebrow as she asked, "And?"

"And it's a bad idea. I need to go home."

"To talk her out of it?"

"Yes."

"I thought you were going to tell me she was pregnant."

"We don't get leave for that."

She smiled slyly. I was a grown man, and she was an open

book. The first page read, *I'd like to fuck you.* "Why should I grant leave for that?"

Emphasis on *why*. Like, *What's in it for me?*

Would she sign leave papers if I agreed?

And if I could confirm that, would keeping Greyson safe be worth destroying my marriage?

No. Not even close.

We weren't there.

The choice between life and death wasn't clear-cut enough to make that deal.

"Because I'm asking."

"You obviously know the rules. You haven't accrued enough time for leave. You don't have a medical emergency. Nobody died."

"On my last deployment, I worked eight days on five hours' sleep. I was pumped so full of amphetamines I was having aural hallucinations. It was my job, and I did it. I've never asked for anything from the army. I did what I had to. Now I have to do this."

"How can you expect me to call your wife coming here an emergency when the army sent you here? Sent me here? Thousands of us are doing our jobs. You're concerned. I get it. But it doesn't hold up."

She was right. I'd have to think of something else.

"Thanks," I said, standing.

"Sorry I couldn't be more helpful." I had my hand on the doorknob when she called out, "Stop."

I turned, hand still on the knob.

"There's something," she said, hands flat on the desk as if this was hard for her. "I can call in a favor to get you leave."

"Okay."

There was more. There had to be more.

"But you have to do something for me."

There it was. A deal. She stood and came around the desk. She was going to try to seduce me, and I was going to refuse her.

"When you're a woman in this position," she said, "you have to deal with a lot of shit."

"Such as?" I took my hand off the doorknob.

"Such as my picture showing up in a Facebook group with the caption 'Who'd like to fuck this one in the ass?' Or getting assaulted in OTS. I'll spare you the rest of the list. But the worst? The body they're all so hot for is high-maintenance." She looked at my crotch and put her hands on her hips. "And what it needs is frowned on because not getting those needs taken care of isn't debilitating enough. No one says anything, but I know men and I know the fucking army."

She was going to touch me. I could sense it. I could use her body to stifle the humming madness. Satisfy the Thing. DeLeon was attractive in all the right ways. Except that she was wrong. I wouldn't have sex with her, not even to protect my wife.

"I'm not going to fuck you."

A smile spread across her face, and it turned into a laugh. "That's your loss. But I need something more practical. I need a procedure, and I can't miss a day of duty for it."

I was so relieved I almost laughed myself. "And you'll call in that favor? It'll get me leave?"

"One hundred percent chance of success."

She went behind her desk, and I sat in the chair across.

Chapter Nine

GREYSON

Four black-and-white monitors. Caden in a small room. Four angles. Frozen in a chair with the word PAUSED over him.

I thought, "I don't want to see this," but I didn't say it.

"Here was the problem," Ronin said with his arms braced against the countertop and his face lit by the four black-and-white monitors. He'd sat me down here after I'd checked in and filled out the forms. "He lied."

I exhaled the first N in *No, he didn't*, but bit the rest back.

Ronin glanced at me and twisted half his mouth into a wry grin. "He was the same about protecting you. It's cute." He hit the space bar on the keyboard.

The word PAUSED went away. Caden sat still, and again I had to stop myself from canceling the whole endeavor. I didn't want to see this, but I had to. I didn't know why. But I had to see it.

"What did he lie about?" I asked.

On the screens, Caden bowed his head, the muscles of his back stretching and contracting as he breathed rhythmically.

"He said he had no history of childhood abuse."

The man on the screen shook. I wanted to lay my hand between his shoulder blades.

"Maybe your question wasn't specific enough," I said.

"Sure."

Caden threw his body against the back of the chair, going rigid as he groaned in mental pain. The waveforms ran along the bottom of the screen with his lips as he said, "No, no, no." His pain was all over his posture. The light vibrated with it.

"It wasn't like this for me," I said.

"The treatment opens doors. Helps you face fears. You're not afraid of anything."

Caden shook his head vigorously.

"No. I am. I'm afraid of plenty."

"Different people, different results. But for victims of abuse, it's more than we can handle here."

Was Caden crying? Oh, Jesus on a ladder, we were separated by space and time. I was powerless in the face of his hurt.

"Is this hard for you to watch, or is it just me?" I asked.

"You get used to it."

"Why didn't you stop him?" My hand hurt. I looked down. I was twisting my fingers like a skein of yarn.

"We had no idea what this was. He gave one-word answers in his questionnaires. I thought he was reliving an experience in Iraq, but then he suddenly got very verbose in his surveys. Told us about some room in his basement."

"Was that six weeks ago?"

Six weeks ago, Damon had done the Blackthorne appointment. Damon would have been verbose and forthcoming where Caden would have finished his questionnaire with a scowl.

"Right about then." Ronin nodded.

On the monitors, Caden's face was buried in his hands, and he was weeping, but his back still expanded with the constant rhythm. He'd come to Blackthorne for me. I'd sold him on it. I'd done this. I'd forced him to dig up things he'd worked hard to forget. I owned every tear he'd shed in that room.

Dr. Frazier, the psychiatrist, knew he had to dig them up.

Greyson Frazier, the daughter of a vet hounded by unexplored trauma, knew the same. But Mrs. Greyson Frazier-St. John had a burden of guilt.

"Why are you showing me this?"

"Because I can't show you the other subject who said they had no history of abuse."

I tapped the space bar, and Caden froze. "Who?"

"You're going to meet them in Baghdad."

"Now that I'm bound by your NDA, let's talk about the patients you sent me."

He leaned back on the counter and crossed his arms. "Let's do something even better. I'll send you the data."

Caden was covered by the word PAUSED, but I knew that under it, he was being crushed by memories he'd never shared with me. I must have been looking at it too long.

"You can get out of the contract, you know. You haven't been paid. You have an out clause."

Caden would be happy. My family would be relieved. I could go back to the hospital and manage the new program the way I'd pitched it.

I tapped the space bar. Caden changed. He stood straight, gripping the arms of the chair, legs spread, mouth open in an angry roar. His eyes were on fire, and he was ready to spring at something only he could see.

My heart stopped, then pounded. He knocked over the chair and lamp. He was terrifying. I'd never seen him angry. Not that angry. Not like an animal.

Was this acceptable to me? And if not, how would going to Baghdad fix it?

I couldn't bear it. I hit the space bar to stop it. "Do you have a boss, Ronin? Or are you running the entire thing?"

"I have lots of bosses, but they prefer it if contractors have one point of contact. That's me. In the army, I'd never be more than a peon for someone. But this program's such a small part of this operation that I get to run it how I want. It's going to change everything."

"Everything?"

Gently, he started the video again. Caden lowered himself to the floor, bowed on his knees, hands in his hair. I wanted to touch the glass to comfort him, but that man was weeks ago and thousands of miles away.

"The way we go to war," Ronin said. "The way we use people. Imagine soldiers coming home with their trauma completely processed. They'd get off the plane mentally clear. Maybe healthier than when they left. All this from a few hours in a dark room? That changes everything." He turned to watch the video with me. "I know we give each other a hard time. But I consider you a friend. So, I'm going to give you some friendly advice."

I had a snappy retort about unsolicited advice rarely

being friendly, but Caden's anguish slowed. Maybe with the *soo-hoo*s I couldn't hear but knew were there. Maybe on his own. He picked up his head, leaving his palms on his face, then lowered them as if he was being born out of his hands.

"I'm listening," I said.

Ronin could give me all the friendly advice he wanted. My mind was made up. Caden needed me.

"Call his CO directly. Tell him about the dissociation. Call it PTSD. You're perfectly qualified to assess him. They'll listen to you. They'll send him home. Then you bail on your contract."

On the screen, my husband stood up straight and righted the chair.

"He'll never forgive me. And I tried that."

"That's what I figured."

Caden buttoned his jacket, all posture and pride. He looked directly at one of the cameras and nodded.

WITHOUT A DOUBLE-BLIND CONTROL GROUP, Blackthorne's bioenergetics breathing data was inconclusive. All correlation. No cause. That would be their excuse when it all went to hell.

I recognized some of names and knew my patients by

their rank and life's experience. Saw my husband and Leslie Yarrow. The ones with the mild dissociation I'd counseled had been going to Blackthorne for the treatment and had found it helpful. As hard as it was to measure mental health, the indicators pointed out that the patients I hadn't counseled who had done the breathing had also done well but not *as well*.

After hours poring over the file, I closed it.

Nice to know I'd helped. Really. But I'd been used. I called Ronin to chew him out, but he wasn't in the office. His cell went to voicemail.

Ronin had been in my life a long time. I enjoyed our constant exchange of witty insults and careless cruelties. His dream of a PTSD-free world was more noble than I'd expected from him, but he was clearly willing to lie to achieve it.

Words aside, his actions were louder and stronger.

He considered me a friend like I considered a roll of toilet paper a best buddy.

"YOU SHOULD HAVE SEEN HIM," I said, hugging my arms as I paced up the Central Park rock and down again.

Jenn had given up on our workout already and was sitting in the grass, touching her toes.

"He was distraught," I continued. "Really, really upset. Deeply. If you weren't me, you wouldn't even know how deeply, but I could see it."

"And now you're more dedicated to going than ever before."

"I can't leave him there."

"You didn't 'leave him there.' He went. He's an adult."

"I can't do this." I was walking back and forth so quickly I was almost at a canter. "Doing nothing is... no. Negative."

"Can you sit please? You're making me anxious."

I threw myself down next to her. "He says he's coming back." I flopped back and faced the canopy of tree branches. The leaves veiled the sky. "I should wait."

"So, you'll wait."

I put my hands over my face to block out the setting sun, but I couldn't block out the tourists, the traffic, or the laughter of children running through the grass. "I am so scared I can't even think."

"Okay, I would ask you what you're scared of, but I already know the answer, so I'm not going to waste your time or mine. You're welcome."

"Thank you." I took my arm off my face and looked at her. "For listening and everything else."

"Close your eyes. I'm working on a meditation for my guys."

"A meditation?" I made an *ick* face.

"Are you going to help me practice or not?"

"Oh, I'm *helping*? Okay." I closed my eyes, grateful to be given something to do. The light through my lids was broken by the shifting shadows of the leaves. I exhaled a small portion of my tension. "I'm ready."

"Focus on my voice."

I took a deep breath and listened, letting the noises of the park slip away, while my friend's voice rose and fell with the rhythm of the earth.

What is your fear?

Call it by its name.

Imagine the fear as an object.

Give it a shape and a color. Put it in a place and leave it there. Observe it. Note its dimensions and its depth. Describe its boundaries and its ability to move... or not.

Proportional to your own body, is it large? Is it heavy? Is the weight balanced? Could you carry it if you needed to? Or does it hold you in one place?

Now imagine it getting smaller.

And smaller.

Make it as small as the palm of your hand.

Note its new dimensions, color, texture. Note what's changed when its size is reduced.

If you haven't already, pick it up.

Hold it in your hand.

Feel the texture and weight of your fear.

Will you put it down and walk away?

Do you put it in your pocket?

Or do you crush it in your fist?

Now that you're holding your fear, the only thing you can't do is nothing.

MOM WAS SITTING in the kitchen, doing the crossword.

"You're up," I stated the obvious.

"Jake called."

"You didn't come get me?"

"Who knew you'd be working so late down there?" She filled in the boxes in blue pen.

"How is he?" Like a teenager, I stood in front of the open

refrigerator, looking for inspiration I couldn't prove was there.

"Fine. He's just north of Baghdad. I told him if he winds up in the hospital, he should ask for his brother-in-law."

"Let's hope they don't have to meet." I got out cranberry juice and closed the door. "Maybe I'll see him though. We can lunch in the Green Zone."

Mom looked at me over her glasses. "I know you feel like once you make a decision, you have to stick to it." She looked back at the paper and added with more than a hint of sarcasm, "I don't know where you got that from."

"Don't put it all on Dad. I have your genes too."

She scanned her puzzle without confirming that she'd stayed in a military life she hated because she'd decided and that was that.

"Energetic sort," she said. "Six letters. Last one is O."

"I'm terrible at this, Ma." I looked over her shoulder at the five empty boxes, last one O, and it came to me. "Dynamo."

"Your father decided he could handle what he came home with." She filled in the letters. "And here we are. You can be like him, but you don't have to be stubborn about it. You can decide to be different."

11 DOWN - *Suitable to be ridden, as a horse.*

"Eleven down is BROKEN," I said, pointing. "I can't be here. Not without him."

18 DOWN - *A secret may be told in one.*

"I never thought of you as dependent on anyone."

She put WHISPER in the boxes before I could say it.

"I'm not," I said defensively. "I'm just..."

32 ACROSS - *Subject of transhumanism.*

"Yes?"

She'd never let me drift off after half a sentence. Like I said, I had genes from both parents.

"Thirty-two across is CYBORG. And I'm not dependent. I'm emotionally insatiable."

"Greed is never satisfied, you know. It'll never let you be happy."

"That sounds like settling, Ma." I tapped the paper. "Nine down I can't figure."

1 + 1 = 3, for example.

She sighed and filled in nine down.

SYNERGY

"Sometimes you have to stop pushing. That's all I'm saying. Let things be the way they are. You could make things worse."

2 DOWN - *Cause for laying low, sometimes.*

"I don't know," I said. "Maybe. I'm just confused now."

She patted my hand and looked up at me. "I don't blame you. It's hard to know what the right thing is."

"It is. It's so hard."

"Think before you leap, and you'll be fine." She put her arm around my waist and pulled me to her. "You're strong and capable. You know that, right?"

"Yeah."

"Good."

She filled in two down.

ACROPHOBIA

AFTER MOM and I finished the puzzle, she went to bed. I read the paper and waited for my call with Caden.

I logged onto Skype at 1:28 a.m. My camera was on. I was a lady with a cup of chamomile tea in the box in the corner.

My heart was lighter, knowing I could call off the whole thing. I didn't want to stay home, and I didn't want to go to Baghdad. Staying home had its benefits, but the upside of going was being with Caden and helping him through this. He needed my body for that, and I was more than willing to let him use it. Maybe a little rough fucking every once in a while would keep him grounded.

Or not.

At one thirty, a horn honked outside. I jumped to reach for the mouse, but it wasn't him.

I would talk to him about whether or not I should go. Full transparency. Now that it was all on the table, he and I could decide together what to do. As a team.

And really, what man in his right mind would choose a war zone over hot sex?

What if the Skype sex wasn't enough to keep Damon's noise at bay?

What if he needed physical contact?

He wouldn't cheat on me, but what if he had to?

At 1:35 a.m., the Skype screen was still dark.

Caden was never late.

All kinds of things could have kept him from the call. Casualties, primarily. Maybe he was working late. Or had a staff meeting. Maybe he'd forgotten.

Maybe he was using another woman's body the way he'd used mine.

Or maybe he was bleeding, dying, dead.

In the dark, quiet night, I was afraid.

Of his death.

Of being alone.

Of my culpability.

Of pushing it all too far.

I was afraid that he was fine and this was the first of many, many times I'd have to identify my fear, close my fist around it, and fail to crush it.

Chapter Ten

CADEN

We sneaked down to an OR in the dead of night like lovers. Naked from the waist down, Colonel DeLeon had her legs spread. In stirrups. I wasn't surprised when she refused general anesthesia.

"Like what you see?" she asked.

"Looks healthy."

"God, this is going to be so good."

"Women usually say that before I scrape out their uterus."

She'd assured me she wasn't pregnant, and from what I could see, she had been telling the truth.

"You're being funny, but getting this bleeding to stop is going to change my life."

"This will pinch a little."

"He said."

She wrinkled her nose when it pinched.

"I would have done this for nothing, you know," I said as I worked.

"As your commanding officer, I don't like pushing for nontransactional favors. Hard limit. We're even. That works for me."

"Works for me too. You're going to feel some discomfort now."

"He said."

I didn't realize I'd forgotten about my Skype with Greyson until the procedure was done and I was snapping off my gloves.

WHEN IT WAS a decent hour in New York, I called our home phone from the base. Her mother picked up.

"Ma?"

"Caden! How are you?"

She was a truly nice person but strong. Stronger than my mother for sure.

"Good. I can't stay on long. Is Greyson there?"

There was clicking and shuffling before she could even answer me.

"Caden?" My wife turned my name into a question.

"I'm coming home, baby."

"When?"

"I don't know. I put in a leave request, and I have it on good authority it's going to be approved."

"But—"

"Just stay there. Can you just stay?"

A pause, bloated and heavy. I could practically hear her hardening her jaw.

"Don't come here," I continued. "Just wait."

"All right. I'll try. But temporary leave doesn't change anything."

"I love you. You know that?"

"Yeah. I do."

We hung up. I knew it changed nothing. I knew it left half the job done. But stalling would have to suffice for now.

WHEN I HEARD the whine overhead, I held on to the

bathroom sink with my toothbrush sticking between my lips and foam dripping down my chin. I knew what it was before I spit. The siren wailed, and a voice over the loudspeaker said to take cover.

I rinsed and dressed quickly. I was an old hand at feeling nothing. As the new Thing got louder, I got better at stuffing my emotions, fears, and reactions away.

We were told the attack had come from a residential area over the Tigris, but that was later. It landed near the presidential palace inside the Green Zone, about two and a half miles from the hospital. The explosions were sharp, pounding, more resonant than when they fell in the Red Zone. The earth shook gently and quickly nine times. One for each mortar.

"That's some minty-fresh breath you have there, Asshole Eyes."

DeLeon and I were smashed against each other with our medical kits on our laps. Two paramedics had smashed us together in the back of the Humvee. A hit to the Green Zone felt personal. It felt like our neighborhood. We weren't staying inside the hospital.

"The better not to kiss you with."

"Your loss!" she shouted as we slammed over a pothole.

"How are you feeling?" I asked.

"Is this my follow-up visit?" The truck whipped around a turn, and we hung on.

"It's all your insurance covers."

She barked a laugh. "I feel great!"

We lost our smiles as we came upon one of the royal palaces. A corner had been knocked off. A block away, a crater opened in the road. People were running everywhere as the Humvee rolled into the blast perimeter. We were out before the truck fully stopped.

A paramedic with soot on his face ran up. "Nurse or doctor?"

"Surgeons," she said. "Both of us."

DeLeon was pulled toward an ambulance while I was taken to a patch of grass where the wounded were being triaged.

"We can't move him."

An Arab boy of about thirteen was sitting up against a tree. He looked fine until I got close enough to see the iron rod impaling his chest. I trotted up to him. There was no blood. His breathing was raspy. The medic called his vitals. She was obviously upset.

"We can't see if it's through the spine."

"You're making the lady sad," I said in terrible Arabic.

He turned to me. He was lucid. Good.

"Do you speak English?" It was my best Arabic phrase, but the boy shook his head. Great.

I tried to see the exit wound, but it was against and possibly through the tree. I ran my hand behind him as he whispered something I couldn't understand.

"Let's get his shirt open." We got the shirt open. Clean entry. Right of the sternum. "I can't determine the angle," I said to the paramedic. "But we have to get him to the OR. If he's pinned to the tree, we have to cut the pipe."

There had been another time an Iraqi had tried to talk to me. Another incident outside the confines of a hospital. It had been...

Dujon. Dujon.

... bad. I hadn't listened.

He whispered again.

I reached behind him again, then heard clearly what he was saying.

"Kunbulla. Is that your name, kid?" I stopped myself and asked, "Your name?" in Arabic as I felt behind him for the pipe's exit.

Around us, people ran, shifted, called out. They prepped a stretcher. Ambulances moved, and the earth turned, but I was focused solely on my probing fingers and the boy's bloody lips.

"Kunbulla." The boy made eye contact, trying to warn me. Apologizing at the same time as he was begging me to save him.

Dujon.

In complete emotional detachment, I remembered. I'd thought she'd been reading my name tape. I'd thought she'd been saying "Dr. John."

Right?

Kunbulla.

Dujon.

My fingers didn't find the place where the bar exited, but a solid mass, squared at the edges, thick as a pack of cigarettes, and as dense as a few metric tons of potential energy.

Qunbula.

Shit.

Chapter Eleven

GREYSON

The computer started making noise after five in the morning. I ignored it, then the night table phone rang.

"Mmh."

"Pick up Skype. I need to see you."

HE WAS FRESHLY SHOWERED. Hair wet. Face scrubbed and shaved.

It was noon there, but his hours had to be all over the place.

"Hi." When his smile turned back down, one cheek stayed red.

"Your face is scraped up."

He put his hand to it. Looked at his fingertips. No blood. The abrasions were too fine.

"What happened?"

"*Qunbula* apparently."

I gasped. "A bomb?"

"Yeah."

"Are you all right?"

"Yeah. I'm fine."

"What happened?"

"I told you."

His look through the screen, across thousands of miles, was as hard and cold as granite. He was quite possibly more beautiful when he was like this than when he was warm with love. But I couldn't compare what I couldn't see.

"You can tell me more without giving away locations. You don't have to say what time or who you were with. Come on. Stop treating me like I don't know the rules. And stop acting like talking to me isn't important."

"Why do you push like this? I just wanted to see your face."

I leaned into the camera. "You have what you want. Plus my unconditional love. Nothing you say is going to scare me."

"That's what I'm afraid of."

The only thing he feared was my fearlessness.

"Did you get the leave?" I asked. "Are you coming back?"

He bit his upper lip and let it pop out. If the resolution had been better, I was sure I'd have seen the dampness of that top lip and a pinkish blur where his teeth had scraped the skin.

"Do you know the Arabic word, sounds like *dujon*?"

"I don't, but my Arabic isn't that good." I wrote it down phonetically. I'd never learned the alphabet. "Is anyone fluent there?"

"Yeah. I'll try them."

"Where did you hear it?"

"It was a suicide bomber," he said.

Where? Medevacs got to the Red Zone after the bombs went off. Was it in the Green Zone? Why were you near him? How did they get in?

Tell me everything.

I couldn't ask any of those questions because he couldn't answer them. I put my hand over my mouth partly in shock, partly to shut myself up.

"A kid," Caden continued. "I was trying to move him. He was... I can't say without giving up the order of events."

"I understand."

"He warned us he was wrapped, and we got away."

"Are you doing all right?"

"I'm fine. I'm sure I'm fine." He was trying to convince himself.

"Tell me."

Those two words broke something in him. Was it the right time to ask? Had something changed?

"It's getting harder," he said. "The Thing. It's different. It's not fear and sympathy. It's anger."

Anger.

What would that split look like if it was allowed to happen?

"Sometimes," he continued, "I think it's all right and I can manage. Then days like today, it's a four-alarm fire."

He bent his body to run his fingers through his hair, turning his face from me for a moment. When he popped back up, I touched the screen where his lips moved.

"We have ways of keeping it down," I said. "But my parents are in the next room."

He looked at his watch. "Dad'll be up soon."

"Can you make it until tonight? I can send them to a movie."

"I'll spend the afternoon deciding where to bruise you."

"I miss you."

"About that...I have some bad news."

"Let me guess." I let my fingers fall from the screen. That needed to be the only expression of disappointment. I couldn't lay more on him. "After today's incident, all R&R passes and nonmedical leaves are withdrawn."

"Baby," he said softly, with a voice that never let me feel infantilized, only loved with the depth one loves their own blood. "I know I can't stop you from doing what you want."

"You didn't marry me for my obedience."

"No, I didn't."

The implication in his tone was that maybe he should have. I let it go. I heard my dad startle awake as if a bomb had just gone off.

"They're up," I said. "I love you, Major."

"I love you too."

We hung up, and I leaned back in my chair. If this Thing was like the old Thing and it was getting louder more frequently, we were back in the old pattern. That period had been awful and unsure, but thinking of the sex made me tingly and wet.

I could stay. I could be that obedient women he hadn't

wanted. I could live in our house and patiently wait for something to happen. Be the bedrock of his chaotic life. It wasn't as if I had nothing to do in New York.

Trusting him came naturally. He'd never presented as a player or a cheat. Even when I'd broken into his locker, I had been ready to have completely misjudged him. But when I considered that if he needed rough sex to stay sane, he'd have to get it, and I'd have to deal with it, my blood curdled. Even the thought of him touching another woman made my palms sweat and my skin prickle with angry heat.

That wasn't on the table. If he'd wanted a milquetoast housewife, he'd had his pick. He'd married me because I pushed his boundaries and let him push mine. But not every limit needed to be tested.

Some lines had to be crossed so others wouldn't be.

Part Two

HEALING

Chapter Twelve

GREYSON

The Phrog's dual rotors buzzed like a swarm of bees. My knuckles were striated in white and pink, and my palms already ached in the center. I kept my eyes on my boots and focused on the pain, feeling it in three dimensions as the shooting ache ran from my right wrist to my shoulder. That helped. Focusing on pain always did.

Nothing had changed. Not for me.

The Iraqi sky was still an infinite blue, but now I knew why that blue had always spoken to me, calling me into it. It borrowed the color from my husband's eyes.

On the way to the Blackthorne offices in Baghdad, I was flooded with fear that I'd drop out of that glassy vacuum and into the solid mass of the earth. Falling away from that blue was falling away from Caden.

"You all right, Frazier?"

I let go of the bench long enough to direct a thumbs-up at Dana Testarino, a PA and fellow contractor. She'd called me by my civilian name, reminding me that I was rankless and unprotected. I had no unit, no position, no military hierarchy. Ronin wasn't there to rib me. Jenn wasn't there to defend me. I was surrounded by a dozen other contractors. We were professional advisors. Experts in our fields. We'd bought our own kits and supplies mostly. I had a cold case strapped to the floor between my feet. It held prefilled syringes of the same compound they gave subjects before the *soo-hoo*s. It was called BiCam145.

"Some of the subjects are active military," Ronin had said. "They're in your files. Major St. John and Specialist Leslie Yarrow have placebo instead of serum because we can't predict how they're going to react."

That was how I got confirmation on the other subject with childhood trauma. That was too bad. I liked her. I didn't want her to suffer, and I didn't want her to see me reenter Iraq as a contractor. I'd thought I didn't have a bone in my body that could feel shame, but I was wrong.

"What is it?" I'd asked.

"It triggers the bioenergetic breathing response. It opens doors. One dose for each subject, premeasured. When the hub touches skin"—through the plastic, he pointed at the rubbery white base of the needle—"it turns blue, and when it's removed, it's self-sealing."

I picked one out of the box. "Why?"

"To make sure the BiCam goes into a body, not another vial."

"To prevent corporate espionage, I presume?"

"Only the latest and best technology."

The latest and best was strapped down tight, and didn't budge when the Chinook swooped around, dropping in a stomach-twisting plunge that brought me closer to my husband and his grounded blue eyes.

BLACKTHORNE HQ OCCUPIED A U-SHAPED, three-story gray brutalist shithouse in the Green Zone. After they took our bags and we were split into military and personnel specialists, we were led to the plaza in the center of the U, next to a dry fountain. Birds chirped. Flowers and tree branches swayed in the breeze. People walked the verandas above, hustling from one place to the next.

Dana sat to my right. A rabbi in his twenties named David was on my left. To the left of him, two men who looked like really tough accountants stood in the shade. Dana and I were partnered. She could administer medications but not diagnose. David was a psychologist. We were the new mental health team.

"It's so nice," Dana said, indicating the trees, the birds,

the infinite blue sky. "You'd never think there was a war going on."

"Yeah," I agreed, but I didn't.

A man in a dark suit approached with a file tucked in his elbow. He was six-four, under two hundred pounds, with a rubbery gait that made him look as though he'd fall down with each step. He was in his fifties, with black hair graying at the temples and a widow's peak.

"Good morning! I'm Ferhad Ghazi." He had a slight accent I couldn't place, and when he opened his arms, I saw a small notebook clipped on top of the papers. Like everyone there, he kept a handgun in a shoulder holster. "Welcome to Blackthorne HQ." He smiled like a salesman. My first instinct was to stand when approached, but I wasn't in the army anymore. "I am your ambassador for the Green Zone office."

HOW FAR AWAY WAS CADEN? What was he doing? Who was he with? He hadn't responded to my flight plans. Had he gotten the email? Did he know I was on the same continent, under the same flag, flying against the same sky?

We shed the accountants on the first floor. They went behind a set of double doors with a guy built like a toolshed. Ferhad brought David, Dana, and me to a large space with dozens of desks. Plants dotted the corners, and motivational posters hung on the white walls. Metal grates over the windows cut the sunlight in half.

"We take pride in our people," Ferhad said as we walked through the room. His voice was smooth and sonorous indoors. "So, we're fully staffed to take care of them. We utilize the military's medical facilities, but as you know"—he nodded to the three of us—"we supplement with our own professionals." He stopped on the other side of the room, at a door with a black box by the handle. "Your ID cards open this area."

He swiped his ID card over the black box. The red light turned green, and the door clacked. He opened it into a reception area. We were introduced to the receptionist and led to a clinic on the other side of the building. Examination rooms. Crash carts. Gurneys. Labeled plastic bins. The only thing that differentiated it from a military hospital was the quiet.

"Your office, Mister Rothstein." Ferhad opened the door to a relatively pleasant office with a desk and worn but cushioned chairs.

"Ladies..." Ferhad took us to the office next door.

Dana was shown her desk in the clinic. My office looked much like David's except for the cold case of syringes sitting ready on my desk.

"We need a refrigerator for this case," I said, pointing at the cooler of BiCam.

"Down the hall," he said.

I heard a loud *ho* from outside. Looking out the window, I saw a man fall off the roof of a four-story building. I gasped and pointed.

Ferhad laughed.

"Did you see that?"

"Yes, yes," he said, waving me to the window on the other side of the room. "Look from here."

He showed me the angle to look from. Another figure jumped, but now I could see them turn midair and rappel from the side of the building. "It's our training facility."

"That's so cool!" Dana exclaimed.

"That's so scary." I was still shaking.

"Yes, but look at the bottom. The blue and yellow?"

At ground level, around the corner of another building, I saw a sliver of blue and yellow stripes, like a pillow covered in a termite tent.

"I see it. Is it an inflatable bag?"

"Yes. So see? You don't have to worry." He pressed my shaking hands in his in a gesture that was not seductive but healing. "Have you seen your quarters yet?"

"Not yet!" Dana was chipper. You'd never have known she'd just been on a military transport.

"We got you a lovely place very close by. Let's get that put away, and I'll have a car bring you."

I HELPED Dana unpack her apartment first, then she helped me. It only took a few hours.

We were in furnished apartments in the Green Zone. The building wasn't new, but it was made from sturdy brick and cracking stucco.

Caden was inside the hospital compound, just under a quarter mile away. It was visible from the third-floor cafeteria at work, and if I could get to the roof of the apartment building, I'd bet good money I could see it.

My bones were made of iron filings, and he was a magnet, drawing my body's brittleness to the surface. Tonight, I'd go there. I'd fight exhaustion and jet lag. I'd see him. Touch him. Smell the coffee grounds and cut grass on his skin. I'd let him have me. I'd beg him to break me.

"You're smiling," Dana said as she wiped down my counter.

"Weird, right?" I put the last of my clothes in the old armoire and closed the door. It was next to the couch because there was no space in the bedroom.

"There's plenty to smile about," she said with the twang of an accent I'd noticed before. "We're making good money. Helping the country. Having an adventure. It's great."

"Where are you from?"

"New Jersey. You?"

"All over. But I landed in New York last."

"We're practically sisters!" Dana opened a can of Coke she'd picked up from the chow hall and leaned on the counter. "Have you seen the guy I'm next door to?"

"Nope."

"Name's Bob Trona, and he's totally hot in this Tom Hardy kind of way."

"Hm. Name rings a bell."

She picked up the novel I'd set aside and flipped to the inside flap. "He was in *Band of Brothers* and—"

"I mean Trona."

Putting a few cups and plates in the cabinet, I saw out of the corner of my eye a piece of paper slip out of the book. She picked it up and gasped so loudly I thought she'd hurt herself.

"What?"

She held up Grady's sonogram with a big shit-eating grin. "This! You're—"

"No, no. That's not me."

She turned it over to look. "The name's all rubbed off."

"It's been through a lot. It came from a soldier in Fallujah I never met. His wife. It's a long story. It's... I don't know. I feel obligated to take it around with me in case I meet a relative or something."

"You're so nice," she said, placing it on the table before turning back to the book.

I smiled. Of course she thought I was nice. That said more about her than it did about me.

I COULDN'T WALK to the hospital alone, especially after dark. Green Zone or not, security was locked down. I caught a ride with a guy armed to the teeth on his way to train the Iraqi Army in counterintelligence. We were stopped twice in the quarter mile and waved along once.

As the hospital came into view, my heart raced. *Soon, soon.*

Caden and I hadn't been separated that long, and I'd thought I was handling it okay, but I wasn't. Not until I stepped through the hospital doors and knew I could see him at any minute did I realize how nervous I was. Not until I was standing in the middle of the admitting room with no idea whom to ask what did I realize I was out of place. I approached the desk.

"Can I help you?" A uniformed woman looked up from a

clipboard. She had a touch of lip gloss and had given her lashes a quick brush of mascara. Her long, straight hair was wrapped tight in the back of her head. It was lighter than mine and matched her eyes. She had a colonel's bird on her collar, and her name tape said DeLeon.

"I'm looking for Dr. St. John."

"Oh, yeah?" She put down the clipboard and looked me up and down.

No leaf cluster or name tape told her who I was. I could have been anyone or no one.

"I'm his wife."

Her gaze flicked over me again, making a different assessment. I held up the Blackthorne ID around my neck.

"Well, it's nice to meet you." She held out her hand. I shook it. "He's in surgery." She called to a black man who was passing, "Stoney. Asshole's wife."

Asshole?

"He's... wait..."

Not an asshole.

But Stoney was shaking my hand, as was a white guy with curly red hair and a short black woman in scrubs. They expressed surprise and shot questions about how long I was going to be around and why I'd come so far to see such an egotistical jerk. Good, solid army ribbing.

"All right," DeLeon said, putting her hand on my shoulder. "Come on. Let's go see what he's up to."

She brought me down a wide, well-lit hallway with a clean tile floor.

"This is much nicer than Balad," I said, letting her know I wasn't some civilian rube. I was jealous of her access to my husband and the place she had in his world.

"It'll do. Were you also there for Fallujah part two?"

"We met right about then."

"And now you're contracting?" The question was loaded, and the answer was worse.

"It's complicated."

"He's a complicated guy." The words left her lips with a touch of bitter syrup.

Something was going on with her. Any doubt I'd had about coming to Baghdad was swept away. I needed to be here.

DeLeon opened the door to a scrub room. "We got a medevac in about two hours ago." She went to the other side of the room to a set of double doors with windows. "He should be finishing up." She peered through. "Yep."

I looked through the other window. Caden's head was bowed over the patient, and his fingers nimbly threaded the wound closed. DeLeon tapped the window. He looked up, saw her first, and smiled warmly.

Too warmly.

When he saw me, the smile dropped into a frown.

Every drop of fluid in my body boiled.

DELEON WAS GONE, leaving me in the scrub room alone. When the surgery was done, the team came in, chattering about the operation. Caden entered last, snapping off a glove and yanking his mask down as if he wanted to say something. But nothing came from his beautiful, generous lips. He held them tight together as mine quivered, locking me in his gaze. The noise of the room was on the other side of a long tunnel.

He was here. No screen. No camera. No microphone. He was a foot away, living, breathing, sucking all the energy in the room. The sun was tucked under the horizon, but in his eyes, it was always daytime.

Wound tight as a man who's been disobeyed for the last time, he peeled off his other glove without looking away from me. "Welcome to Baghdad, baby."

HIS SPACE WAS the size of a dorm room. Still in scrubs, without saying any more than "Follow me," he'd led me across a narrow street to a heavy door, up a flight of stairs, and down a hall that echoed my footsteps.

He had a twin bed made so tightly I could have bounced a quarter on it. A sink with a mirror. A cheap pressed-wood wardrobe. His trunk. A desk with a plastic chair. He closed the door to his room and locked it but didn't turn to me. He just kept his hand on the lock.

"Greyson." The muscles of his back were defined against the fabric stretching across it.

"Caden." I held my hand out to put it between his shoulder blades and draw it down to his ass but pulled it back before touching him.

"You're here."

"I told you I was coming."

He put his forehead on the door. "I'm so disappointed I can barely think."

"I know."

"In myself."

"It's not your fault." Taking a deep breath, I put my hand on his back.

He curved away, turning around quickly, as if I'd stung him. "That's not what I meant. It's all locked up. I don't feel anything. I'm detached from myself. And when I see you, all I can think about is how you're the cure for everything that's wrong with me." His hands flexed open and closed as if they were ready to grab something and hold it tight enough to crush it.

"I am the cure," I whispered, unbuttoning my shirt. "Take your medicine."

Watching me unbutton, he considered, then put his hand on my bare skin. "I want to lay everything at your feet." He took me by the throat, digging his thumb and middle finger into each side of my jaw. "Leave it all on the table."

"Take it. Leave it." I undid the last button, exposing my simple white bra. He tightened his grip just enough to see if I was scared. I wasn't. I was a node of firing desire. A liquid conductor of sexual electricity. "I'm yours."

He murmured close to my face. I wanted a kiss so badly I was drunk with the need for it, but his lips didn't touch mine.

"Take off your clothes." He put upward pressure, making his hand the one thing to unbalance me and the one thing to keep me upright. I undid my pants on my tiptoes as he murmured to my face, "You're going to break without a sound. Not a word. Not a scream. If you want me to stop, you better say it quietly."

My pants fell around my ankles. I still had my boots on.

"Do you hear me?"

I nodded as much as I could.

"Say stop."

I shook my head. The choice was enough to drive more fluid between my legs.

He let me go and leaned back, taking me in, then walked behind me. I felt his sky-colored eyes along the length of my body, from the hair coming out of its ponytail to the pants pooled around my ankles. He unhooked my bra and slid it off, then yanked my underwear down around my thighs.

"I can smell your cunt," he whispered into the back of my neck. "It's apples." He laid his lips on the muscle between my neck and shoulder. "It's delicious, just like your pain."

With that, he bit me slowly. His teeth were all pleasure with an increasing tension. I gasped, swallowing a cry. With the same slow control, he reduced the pressure of the bite.

"Caden," I whispered, feeling him getting his cock out of his scrubs.

"Are you telling me to stop?" He wrapped his arm around me, grabbing a tit at the base and working up to the nipple.

"No."

"I need something from you."

"Anything."

"If I go too far and you say stop... if I don't, I want you to bite. Kick. Punch me in the face. These walls are thin." He twisted the nipple, brushing his erection against me. "If you scream, someone will hear you. If I don't stop, you need to scream."

I nodded. With his other hand, he pressed four fingers between my legs, opening me. He ran his lips to my other shoulder and made a matching bite with excruciating slowness as he circled his hand over my clit. The pleasure was overwhelming, but the pain was too much to let the orgasm loose. I bit back a cry. Tears dropped down my cheeks.

"If you have something else to say," he said when he released my flesh, "do it now. Quietly." His hand stopped moving.

"Have you been faithful to me?"

I felt him shake his head, and taking that as a no, my tears increased.

"Oh, baby." He came around to face me. His magnificent cock held down the waistband of his scrubs and his hand cupped my chin. "There's no one who can love me like you do."

"So, you didn't?"

"Never."

I tilted my face to kiss the palm of his hand. He stayed in the caress for a moment, then kicked off his shoes and twisted out of his shirt. Then he leaned down and unlaced my boots. He sat on the chair. I stepped out of my boots and pants, fully naked.

"Sit here facing me." He patted his thigh and maneuvered me until I straddled his leg, then he put a hand on each of my hips and moved me back and forth. My wetness got all over his leg, helping me slide against it. "Make yourself come."

He leaned back and watched me like a casual observer. When I put my hand on his dick, he moved it away. "I was going to make you do this when we Skyped again."

I gripped the arms of the chair and moved against him. When I was close, he pinched my nipples so hard I choked on a scream.

"Come on, Greyson," he said softly. "This is nothing. I haven't even fucked your ass yet."

I came at the thought, bending back and lurching forward again, clamping my lips shut. He let my tits go and turned me around until he was fucking my pussy from behind. I made a sharp *hm* when he entered me, and he groaned low in this throat.

I felt something cold and wet on my butt. A lotion or cream. His hands were everywhere, spreading it over his cock, my ass.

"Quietly now." He pulled me up and put the head of his dick on my anus. "Down at your own pace."

I lowered myself onto him. It had been a long time, and I

was tight, stretching around him. I whimpered, rose, dropped again.

"You're so fucking hot. So tight. I love it when you stretch open for me."

Without crying out, I jerked down, impaling myself on half of his length. I stopped and breathed heavily, getting used to his size.

"I love it when you hurt for me." He reached around to rub my clit, and I bore down on him until he was buried. "Fuck it, Greyson. Fuck it silently, and I'll let you come."

The pain was gone, leaving only the feeling of being stretched to my limit for him, pushed against boundaries, doing more than I thought possible. He rubbed me furiously as I fucked him, and we came together in a silent whirlwind.

I leaned back, and he cradled me in his arms, whispering, "I wish you hadn't come. I'm so glad you came."

Chapter Thirteen

CADEN

When I'd hurt her and she cried, the buzz had sighed, draping itself over me like a bedspread thrown wide over a mattress. I held it on a leash but let it get its satisfaction.

The raw potential of the Thing had rumbled behind a thin wall. Pure, uncontrolled rage. A hunger for destruction. Tearing her apart, destroying her, all those were figures of speech until I had to hold back what it wanted.

The leash was strong enough, but for how long?

———

WE BOTH NEEDED A SHOWER, and mine was down the hall. I was off duty, and leaving the hospital compound was generally overlooked if it didn't interfere with work and I showed up for emergencies.

So, I took Greyson back to her place on the Blackthorne compound.

The cracked stucco building behind an eight-foot cinderblock wall had four doorbells and a keypad. Behind the iron gate was a small yard with swinging lanterns strung between the house and the perimeter poles over a beat-up table, with half-used candles and two plastic cups, surrounded by mismatched but functional chairs.

"I've only been here once," she said in the dark, "so give me a minute." It wasn't dark for long. Motion-sensor lights flicked on when we passed entry doors. "This is me. Number three."

The door was a hundred years old, but the keypad next to it was brand new. She waved her card past the laser. It beeped and clicked open.

"Oh, hi!" A woman's voice came from behind, and I spun around to get between Greyson and whatever danger my brain had decided was creeping up behind us. It was a woman in her late twenties with a blond bob and bangs. "Sorry about the mess." She picked up the plastic cups, and I relaxed.

"It's fine," Greyson said. "Dana, this is my husband, Caden. He's over in the hospital."

"Nice to meet you."

We shook hands. Her nails were manicured. That wouldn't last long.

"Ferhad came by. He put an envelope under your door."

"Thanks," Greyson said. "See you tomorrow."

"Bye!" Dana said merrily and skipped off.

"She could stand to cheer up a little," I said.

"Don't give her any ideas." My wife leaned into the door, pushing it open.

As promised, a white envelope was on the floor.

OUR FIRST NIGHT IN BAGHDAD, I stayed in her apartment. It was on the upper floor and came furnished with linens and sheets, like a hotel.

With the anger placated, I felt more in control. I didn't have to lock everything away to keep it quiet. Before I'd given her pain, my emotions had been locked away. Afterward, I faced the fact that I was upset that she'd come, and I was also relieved to see her.

With her, even insanity felt controllable. With her, I was strong enough, good enough, capable enough. She made a shitty world come up flowers and rainbows. She didn't erase the cruelty and ignorance, but when she was in the room, I couldn't deny that as ugly as shit got, beauty and perfection existed. The Universe with a capital U had something to aspire to.

She sat between my legs in the bathtub, her back to my chest. Her trapezius muscles were beat to shit where I'd bitten them.

"Dana's licensed to administer meds but not prescribe." Greyson told me about her job. "And she needs MD oversight. So, we've written up all the scripts in case of emergency."

I kissed her shoulder. "This might hurt when you lift your arm."

She leaned back against me. "It'll remind me of you."

"So what's the point of the shots?" I asked.

"It's for soldiers who've done the treatments you did."

"Really?"

"It reproduces the effect of the breathing exercises. Opens the doors of the mind so memories that cause mental trauma can be detached from negative emotions. If it works, it's years of treatment packed into a few days."

"And you believe this works?"

She sighed and leaned her head back against my shoulder, stretching her beautiful body against me. She pointed her toes against the far wall. "I don't know. I know how it affected you, and there's a sense to it."

"You know how it affected me, do you?"

She turned, kneeling between my legs. "You never told me the breathing was so hard on you." Her lashes were blacker when wet, stuck together like pen marks around her chocolate eyes.

I wiped a cluster of bubbles from her cheek. I shrugged. "I said I'd do the treatment. That means I do the treatment. If I complained, you'd either tell me to stop or feel guilty about it."

"You didn't tell them about your father."

"They didn't ask."

"They didn't ask about childhood abuse?"

She was working hard to be nonconfrontational, but some things were confrontations no matter how you phrased them.

"What do you want from me?"

"I want to know why you didn't tell them."

"I wasn't abused. My mother was."

She bit her lips back as if that would confine what she wanted to say. I knew what it was. Abuse of the mother is abuse of the child. But I didn't agree and I wasn't arguing about it.

She put her hand on my chest. "I'm on your side."

"I know. But it's my life. I'll characterize it the way I

want. And not to change the subject"—I help up my finger—"you should have stayed home."

"It's my life." She repeated my words, then bit her lower lip against a smile that demilitarized the entire subject.

I put my hands on her hips and pulled her to me. "It's *our* life."

I sealed my answer with a deep kiss.

THE PRAYER CHANT woke me at dawn. Greyson was next to me, her hair spread over the pillow like a veil.

"I never thought I'd hate prayer," she said, eyes still closed.

"I have to go anyway." I kissed her cheek. "I'm on rotation."

She got up on one elbow. "I'm sore everywhere."

"Good." I got out of bed and put on my pants. My dick had its own sore spot after entering her so many times the night before. That was good too.

She sat with a groan and stretched as I got my shirt on. "You're doing the walk of shame."

"I've never been less ashamed of anything."

I kissed her. When I tried to pull away, she held me back.

"I love you, Caden."

"I know you do. No one would do such stupid shit unless they were in love."

Chapter Fourteen

GREYSON

There were a few cups and plates in the cupboards but no coffee. Without a commissary, I'd have to get it at a local Green Zone vendor.

The envelope was on the table by the front door. Flipping it over, I saw a sticker over the flap. CONFIDENTIAL. I tore it and slid out the stapled pages.

CLEAN MINDS PROJECT
List of subjects.

The cover letter gave instructions for use of BiCam145. Each was marked with the name and serial number of the recipient. No substitutions. No transfers. No changes in dose. To be administered by the psychiatrist or physician's assistant on staff after a traumatic event. Subject to be monitored closely afterward. Surveys given before and after. I knew all this already.

Under the letter was a list of names. I flipped to S.

Caden was there with an asterisk. So was Yarrow. The back-page footnote was clear.

placebo recommended.

There was a quick, demanding knock at the door. Maybe Caden had forgotten something? I peeked out the window.

A dark-haired, fully-armed man in US Army-issued camouflage. His back was to me, but I'd have recognized that cocky posture anywhere.

I whipped the door open and leapt into his arms. "Jake!"

He held me up as if I was twelve all over again and he was my strapping big brother. "Punky!"

He spun me around.

"Oh my God," I said when he dropped me back to the floor. "So long. It's been—"

"Since your wedding." He smiled, drinking in the sight of me like a thirsty man. "I missed your crazy ass."

"Come in!"

"I only have a minute unless I want to go AWOL."

"I have to get to work. Come, come." I ushered him in and closed the door. "Sit. God, you look like such a *man*."

He had always been handsome, but he'd earned some toughness around the cheeks and a few lines around his eyes.

"You look skinny." He clearly didn't approve.

"Don't get me started. Tea? There are mint leaves growing in the front. I picked a few."

"Sure. They set you up nice."

"Perk of the job." I filled the teapot and plugged it in. "You should see the office."

"And you don't get bossed around as much."

I stuffed leaves into two glass cups. "Oh, there's plenty of bossing around. I heard you got your silver bar?"

"Again."

Jake had been demoted back to butterbar twice. He followed orders but had a habit of doing it in whichever way he found personally appropriate.

"Well, you'll keep it this time." I sat across from him while the teapot did its work. "How have you been? And get right to it."

"You never liked small talk."

"Not from you."

"Are you going to psychoanalyze me?"

"Yep. And we have about fifty minutes. No charge."

He leaned back in the chair, legs spread, hands linked over his chest. "I shouldn't have taken this deployment. It was stupid."

"Why?"

"I could ask you why you came back."

"You could. You first though." I was on the edge of my seat, not for the answer but for the comfort of his voice.

"Remember that time you called me from that punk club? The Spot or something?"

I did but barely. I'd been drunk, eighteen, and frightened our parents would be mad. He'd picked me up and taken me home.

"The Red Spot, and it wasn't punk. It was New Wave."

"The night before you enlisted."

A wave of panic went through me, as if talking about this was a toxic sea I was being asked to jump into.

"Let me check on the tea." I bounced up. The electric pot was already hissing. "Sugar?"

"No, thank you. Do you know, I've never felt as useful as that night? Every time I come here, I think I'm going to be doing something I can be proud of, and I'm wrong every fucking time."

I poured the tea. "You're useful. You just can't see the big picture. None of us can."

"Maybe the picture's too big for me."

I was supposed to listen without judgment or direction, but I could still feel the sulfuric sting of the toxic sea and changed the subject. "What about a woman in your life?" I poured hot water over mint leaves. "Anyone?"

He shrugged. "This and that. How's the moms and dads?"

"We did a little reminiscing when they came to visit. I found out about the talk you had with Scott Verehoven's father."

A smile spread across his face. "Yeah."

"That was gross, Jake." I handed him his glass.

"But I felt useful. See, that's the key. I wasn't looking for shit that wasn't there or securing a road we'd lose in a month. I could rescue a damsel in distress."

"Really, Jake?" I tucked myself into the chair across from him, cradling my glass. "That's sad. You could have let the lawyers take care of it."

"Fuck the lawyers." He blew on the tea. "We take care of business. It's the Frazier way"

That was how I'd found myself in Baghdad. Just taking care of business. That was why Jake had been bumped down to butterbar twice. We were a family of people completely unsuited to the military, yet there we were, three generations in.

I raised my glass cup. "To the Frazier way."

He clicked his cup to mine. "The Frazier way."

"I missed you," I said.

"I missed you too. Now tell me what the fuck you're doing with Blackthorne? You came for your husband?"

I sighed. We had thirty more minutes, and I feared we'd spend it talking about me. "I did. I came for him. He didn't want me to, but I did it anyway."

He knocked his scalding tea back in a single gulp before clicking the glass on the table.

"That's how we roll," he said, and I knew that as much as he didn't approve of my decision, he'd never deny it was the right one.

DAYS WENT by without word from Caden. If I put my cheek to the window in my office, I could see the hospital. The soreness in my shoulders and between my legs faded. Whenever I saw a Blackhawk land on the pad by the hospital, I wondered if he was on it.

I counseled my fellow contractors in the mornings over marital and money issues. The afternoon's paperwork was ten percent less odious than the army's and geared more toward ass-covering than record-keeping.

The BiCam145 serum inside the "latest and best"

syringes had been filed away in a refrigerator, but it weighed on me. I wanted to see if it worked. Through my work counseling Blackthorne's patients, I'd unknowingly had a small part in its development, and I felt responsible for it.

Ferhad's lunch tray was pushed to the side. He ignored Dana and me in favor of the little notepad he carried on his clipboard. He was a poet and could write it in the middle of a conversation.

"This is terrible," I said, dropping the rest of my chicken salad sandwich onto the plate.

"I hear it's harder to get food and stuff into the Green Zone since the bomb attack," Dana said before finishing the last of her sandwich. In addition to being a font of good cheer, she was a first-class news-gatherer.

"Everyone's on edge," Ferhad said, pencil still moving. "Zone isn't as green as it used to be."

"The Zone's always greener on the other side of the wire." Dana giggled at her own joke.

"They strapped bombs to a child." Ferhad put down his pencil. "If the doctor trying to help him didn't speak Arabic, another dozen would have been dead."

"He—"

—*doesn't actually speak it.*

No one needed to know what Caden spoke or didn't.

"What does *dujon* mean in Arabic?" I asked. "I speak a little, but I've never heard it."

"I don't know if it's Arabic," he said.

"Oh." I glanced at Ferhad's poetry. "I thought you were writing in Arabic."

"This is Sorani. It's Kurdish."

"Ah, I'm sorry to assume."

He waved it off. "It's a fine thing. *Dujon*"—he said it with a different inflection—"is Kurdish too. It means 'I'm pregnant.'"

THAT NIGHT, I reconstructed the conversation where Caden had mentioned the word. He had been talking about the suicide bomber, but I was sure he'd said it was a boy.

Who had been pregnant? And when?

Maybe Caden had gotten the word wrong and I'd made it worse. Maybe it was a different word altogether. There might have been no mystery there, but it nagged at me. Right next to the place where I doubted I should have come to Iraq at all.

I wasn't watching over my husband. Wasn't caring for him. I still missed him. I still didn't know if he was in danger, and even if he was, I had no way of preventing it.

In the middle of the night, I curled up inside myself, wondering if I knew what I was doing at all. I assumed I was wide awake until the phone rang.

"Dr. Frazier. This is Colonel DeLeon."

I shot up to a sitting position as if I'd been administered a day's worth of cortisol. "Caden?"

"No, no. Hold up."

"What?"

"It's not Caden. Old Asshole Eyes is just fine. I'm calling you as the psychiatrist on staff at Blackthorne."

I put my hand to my forehead and tried to think calm thoughts. "Okay. Sorry. Go ahead."

"I have two patients here. Just got pulled out of a fire this past morning. Both their files got a big note on them. I'm supposed to call you guys if they're showing signs of traumatic stress."

"Right. Yes." I swung my legs over the side of the bed. "Can I have their names?"

"What's this about?"

"They were part of a DoD-sponsored protocol. I'll bring releases."

"You better." She gave me the names.

I HANDED DeLeon the releases and a pamphlet describing how I didn't have to tell her shit either because or in spite of the fact that Blackthorne was paid by the Pentagon.

She stuck her tongue in her cheek as she flipped through the pamphlet. "This is bullshit. You know that, right?"

"If I were in your shoes, I'd say the same thing."

"What's in the case?"

"It's confidential."

"Yeah, well, I'm not going to do chem tests on it. I want to look at it." She crossed her arms. "They're in my hospital. I could tell you to just fuck off."

She could, as a practical matter. If I wanted to challenge her, I'd have to make a series of phone calls I didn't want to waste time on. I put the box on the desk and opened it.

Without asking, she pulled out the plastic bag with the syringe numbered for Specialist Gregory Linderman. "What is it?"

"It's new. Experimental. And it partners with a lot of work he's already put in." Implying she owed it to the man to let him finish what he'd started.

"Why's there only one?"

I reached into the side pocket for the placebo marked with Leslie Yarrow's number. I didn't want to get them mixed up.

"Prefilled? They don't trust you to do your job?"

"Less transfer from container to container means less chance someone from Halliburton will get their hands on it."

She handed back Linderman's syringe. "If you weren't married to Asshole Eyes, this wouldn't fly, you know."

"If you weren't his CO, I'd throat punch you for calling him Asshole Eyes."

She whooped a laugh, pointing at me after she clapped. "Wifey for the win. Come with me."

Chapter Fifteen

CADEN

Fighting through a barrage of fire and explosives for control over the blocks around some royal palace or another, they'd found a basement of children tied to hooks in the cement floor. All were malnourished. Three were dead.

Linderman was a mess. He'd come off the chopper with a broken leg an Eagle Scout could have fixed, but he was shaking so hard we couldn't set the bone. We gave him enough sedative to stop the shaking, but when it wore off, he stared in the middle distance with a notable lack of affect.

Yarrow seemed better at first. Burn wounds on her left side. They'd scar but heal. She started crying the next morning and couldn't stop.

"What the fuck?" On the computer, DeLeon had been

scanning their files before calling in the psychiatrist. She picked up the phone. "I'll say hi to Wifey for you."

I looked over her shoulder. Blackthorne subjects.

I wondered if I had the same red box in my file.

I wondered about the children in the basement.

I wondered if there had been blood from the dead ones and if it smelled of copper in the darkness.

I COULDN'T GET the children in the cellar out of my mind. The cold floor. The weight of the dark. The smell of blood and the dying ones.

The anger Greyson had helped me satisfy two days ago faded into consciousness, and I was left with the buzz of emotions as a separate thing fighting to push through the membrane of my defenses and swallow me in blackness.

It wanted her. It was drawn to her tears and her broken skin.

My better self needed her. She anchored me.

I hadn't seen her in days, which was nothing. But at the same time... too long. I kept half an eye on her as long as she was sitting in the ICU.

"How old are you?" DeLeon asked.

"Thirty-seven, why?"

"You're like a smitten teenager." She pointed at Greyson, whom I'd surreptitiously been watching through a window.

From afar, I'd watched her speak to Linderman for an hour with little response. She'd talked to their CO about what they'd experienced and taken notes. She waved when she saw me, and I nodded then pretended to ignore her. Now she was taking out the syringe, talking to Miss Cheerypants.

"For Chrissakes." DeLeon rolled her eyes. "Can you go over there and make sure she knows what she's doing?"

"She knows what she's doing."

"Go watch her anyway before I puke."

"I'M SUPPOSED TO WATCH YOU," I said as Greyson unwrapped Linderman's shot.

He was still in his fugue in the ICU, one room over. Dana had scurried off to take notes on Yarrow.

"I'm capable of giving an injection. You should know that." She checked the prefilled amount with the amount on her sheet.

"How's he doing?"

"Bad. And she was one of mine, from New York." She shook her head slightly. She cared about her people, and this bothered her.

"They're both going home," I said.

"Good. What they saw. What happened." She put the needle in a tray. "I'd be traumatized."

"Yeah. Me too."

"Caden."

"Don't. I'm fine."

Still as a statue holding a metal tray with a single syringe, she clearly didn't believe me.

"Go," I said. "Before they send him home without your damn shot."

She went, and I walked behind her. She was the light in the infinite darkness. The fiery star in the blackness of space. With her, there were no cellars.

And yet, the cellar wanted to eat her alive.

I WATCHED from a safe distance as she administered Linderman's injection. The base of the needle turned blue, and she placed it on the tray.

Then she went to talk to Yarrow, and I still watched her—

not because DeLeon had told me to, but because I couldn't take my attention off her. She sat at Yarrow's bedside for over two hours, leaning forward the entire time as if she didn't want to miss a single word.

That beautiful face, in a cry of pain. My pain. Pain I took from her. A part of me knew I was deep inside the darkest parts of the chasm I carried, but there was so much pleasure there for both of us.

DeLeon came up next to me and spoke softly. "Go look at Linderman."

"Why?"

"Shut up and do it."

I tore myself away from Greyson and went to the ICU, where Linderman was sitting up in bed, eating a cup of Jell-O, and joking with one of his buddies. He was animated, warm, seemingly unbroken.

It was as if the children in the cellar had never happened.

Could she erase the cellar for me? Could she make me normal?

Did I want to be?

I should have been happy for Linderman, but I didn't know whether to envy him or resent him, so I cut off all my feelings about it and added it to the buzz that tried to push its way through me.

Chapter Sixteen

GREYSON

The sadness worked its way through Yarrow's body, wracking it with sobs. For up to ten minutes at a time, she couldn't form words. I sat with her and waited every time. I liked her. Whether or not I should have come to Iraq for Caden was a moot point. This woman needed a familiar face. She made it all worth it.

"Oh, man," she said in an interstice between crying jags. "I'm so glad you're here."

"Do you want me to arrange a call to Molly?"

"Not yet. I don't want her to hear me like this, and I can't... I can't tell her about those kids." She folded a tissue into a square, absently creasing the edges. "She got upset when I told her about the bloody face. Couldn't sleep for a week."

The face was a man in her unit who'd died from a head wound. The had blood covered his face, his teeth, the whites of his eyes as he screamed. She'd stayed with him as he died and brought him home with her.

"When you were working with me, you said there had been this feeling of being watched. Like someone else was always with you."

"Yeah." The crying had slowed now that she was distracted.

"You were doing treatments at Blackthorne for it."

"I wasn't supposed to tell anyone."

"I know. But..." I held up the contractor ID that hung around my neck.

"Right. So, you know about it."

Caden and Yarrow had experienced childhood abuse. If Caden's work in the black room was painful, Yarrow's might have been too. But outside that room, my husband's results had been remarkable. The psychic overload had slowed. Had he been able to keep up with it, he would have had enough respite to work through the issue normally.

I'd been taught the timing and tone of the breathing in New York. I could help her even with a placebo.

"Did the sessions help?" I asked.

"Yeah. They did actually."

"I know it's busy in here and the lights are bright, but can you do the breathing if I guide you?"

"I think so."

"If it gets too much, squeeze my hand, and I'll bring you out."

"Okay."

I put my hand under hers. "You're going to be all right."

"When I close my eyes, I see them."

"I'm going to give you other things to see."

"Okay. I trust you."

"Close your eyes and pretend you're in the Blackthorne offices. Walk through the halls. Your arm hurts where they gave you the shot. The tech lets you into the small room. See the yellow light of the lamp. The way it makes the black walls look dark gray. You sit and feel the chair under you. You see the cameras. They make you feel safe because you know you're not alone."

Her face relaxed, and her breathing got shallow and clear of sobs.

"The tech hooks up your monitors and leaves. The door clicks closed behind her. You're comfortable and safe." I waited, watching to make sure she believed she was safe. "Begin the circular breathing with me. *Soo-hoo. Soo-hoo.*"

YARROW WAS RESTING. She'd sobbed her way through the breathing, but it wasn't fear or powerlessness. It was cathartic. She came out of it renewed enough to call her wife and give her the good news. She was going home.

Dana came up to me as I was leaving the ICU.

"Hey, you signed off on all these." She handed me a clipboard with the signed releases. "We still have one in the bag."

"I didn't give her the shot yet."

"Why not?"

"It's a placebo." I flipped through the pages, signing. "I wasn't wasting time with it when she was in real pain. I'll give it to her before she leaves."

"Okay. Hey, have you seen Linderman?"

"I was about to go check on him." I handed back the clipboard.

"It's like a miracle."

DELEON HAD WOKEN me at dawn. It was now midmorning. I was hungry and tired.

I was also elated.

Ronin had used me. He was a complete shit. Always was and always would be. But after seeing Linderman, I knew this thing worked. Long-term effects remained to be seen, but in the short term, it fucking worked.

When Caden and I had been deployed together, a million years ago in 2004, we'd had inconsistent schedules. They'd been posted on a white board behind the nurses' station. If either of us noticed a crack of time where we could eat a meal together, we'd put a red dot by the other's name for the cafeteria or a T to meet in his trailer.

Baghdad had a similar setup. I didn't have my schedule posted, but there was a red R by Caden's. He was calling me.

HE OPENED the door and stood to the side so I could come in, then closed it behind me. I spun around and kissed him so hard and so fast it took him a second to catch up.

"It works," I said, peppering him with kisses. "All of it. It works."

"What—?"

"The breathing. The shot. Everything." I dropped my voice, remembering the thin walls. "God, I need you to fuck me now."

He threw me on the bed and stood over me, his cock tenting his pants. I hadn't taken a second to look at him before kissing him, but at that angle, I saw a shadow of Cold Caden's expression. The Not Damon. Always there, even with Damon gone.

I toed off my boots as he undid his belt.

"Caden," I said, "if Damon's gone, was he replaced with something else?"

He froze. I'd hit on something I hadn't known I was aiming for.

"Tell me," I said, opening my voice to accept an answer I wouldn't like hearing.

"There's something." He whipped his belt out of the loops. "It doesn't have a name."

"Damon didn't have one at first."

He undid his button and zipper. "This one's too angry to have a name. It wants to destroy everything. It's dumb and pissed off, and I have a handle on it."

"So, I shouldn't be scared?" I didn't feel scared. I felt sexy and vulnerable. Fiercely protected from and by a raging animal.

"I'll let you know." He bent over and yanked down my waistband, whispering with a rumble, "Get these off. Turn on the bed and spread your legs wide. I want to see how wet you are."

He got up and opened his trunk as I slid out of my pants. The lid kept me from seeing what he was getting, so I turned to align with the bed and spread my legs.

"Knees up," he said, his gaze still in the trunk. "Show me you want it."

Tucking my hands under my knees, I brought them to my chest. The air cooled where I was wet, letting me know how exposed I was.

Caden stood, holding two clamps and latex surgical tubing. He looked my naked body up and down as if he were solving a problem. There was desire in it, but it was a calculation, not a passion. He was going to own my body with precision. "Hands over your head."

I released my knees, but kept them up, and crossed my arms over my head. Coming between my eyes and the window's light, he leaned over, casting me in shadow. He folded my arms together, inner wrist to inner wrist to protect my old injury, and wrapped the tubing around them. I smelled the latex as it snapped, his ground coffee scent as he leaned close to me. His dog tags hung outside his T-shirt, dangling from his neck and onto my cheek. The knee closest to him was tucked under his arm, folding me tighter into vulnerability.

"I can't welt your ass, or everyone will hear," he said. "But you'll cry anyway. You'll cry like you've never cried."

This was Cold Caden.

I could fix this man, but when he talked like that, I didn't want to.

"Always make me cry," I said as he tied off the tubing. He looked down at me, mouth firm. "Always find my edge."

"No talking." He held up the surgical clamp so I could see it. "Not unless you're telling me to stop. Understand?"

"Yes."

He placed the business end of the clamp at the top of my forehead and ran it down my nose, my throat, making a path of tension over my chest before circling a hard nipple.

"The pain comes when the clamp is released and the blood flow rushes back." He ran it around the other breast. "Do you want it on your nipple?" he asked softly, drawing it over my belly. "Or your clit?"

I clenched when he ran the tip over the nub jutting between my lips. I wasn't supposed to answer unless I wanted him to stop, and I wanted him to keep going. My breathing got sharp and hard as he made a path inside my thighs, considering the red line it left in its wake.

"I saw Linderman." He unbent my leg and ran the edge of the clamp behind my knee to the bottom of my foot. "And I saw you with Yarrow." He changed the pressure from a tickle to not-quite-painful. "You want to do that to me. You want to make me your patient."

"No, I..." My sentence fell away when he took the clamp off me. "Don't stop, but that's not true."

He calculated, blue eyes flicking side to side across my defenseless body. "Let's save something for later."

So businesslike he could have been closing off a bleeding artery, he clamped my nipple. I clenched my jaw until the pain subsided, then he did the other one and stood over me as I writhed. He peeled off his shirt and stepped out of his pants until he was wearing nothing more than his dog tags.

Wedging himself between my legs, cock along the length of my seam, he kissed my cheek and murmured, "Your pain is beautiful." He jerked his hips to rub his shaft along my clit and back down. "If you fix me, will I still think so?"

I didn't know. I didn't care. I couldn't give him the shot, but I also couldn't explain that right then. I just wanted his dick in me. I was pulsing for him, trying to suck it inside me, twisting to get his skin against the sensitive pink between my legs. Burning up, skin prickling—a few more strokes and I was going to come.

He adjusted the trajectory of his cock, sliding it into me, stretching me like a hand in a glove. Moving slowly, we built the foundations of my orgasm without releasing it.

Caden put the tip of his nose to mine. "You ready?"

I nodded furiously. He pushed deep inside. Down to the

root. I grunted with the impact, then the extra stimulation blossomed when he moved against me. It flowered into... excruciating pain as he removed the clamps. The orgasm rode the edge of the pain, skipping over it like a rock on a lake before it rose in a tidal wave.

Knowing I couldn't suppress the cry, he pressed his hand over my mouth and fucked me faster. I gave the orgasm to his palm, arching my body to be closer, ever closer to him.

"I WANT the shot you gave Linderman," Caden said quickly, as if he didn't want to think too hard about it.

The afternoon sun shot through the window grates. We were dressed and satisfied. He was himself again, the two halves joined by my pain.

"I can't."

"Why not?"

I took a deep breath. He hated talking about his childhood. "It's for when you look like Linderman or Yarrow. Not for random Tuesdays."

"I'll have to get traumatized then."

"Hush, you." I poked him in the chest, and he held me tight.

"I want you to traumatize me." He tickled me, and I laughed.

"Stop or you'll traumatize me." I pushed him away, but he caught me and threw me on the bed, laughing, kissing my face and neck.

The knock at the door interrupted us.

He snapped his head around. "What?"

"Um, hey!" It was Dana. "Is Dr. Greyson in there?"

Caden opened the door. My PA hugged a clipboard.

"What's going on?" I asked her.

"It's Yarrow."

"FORTY-FIVE MINUTES AGO," Dana said as we strode through the hospital doors. "She seemed fine."

"Why did you give her the BiCam without me?"

"They had a space on the next chopper out. I knew you wanted to give it to her before she left. I came by your husband's door, but the bed was squeaking."

I'd been warned about the thin walls and was about to give her a talking-to about procedures when I heard the screams. We ran down the hall.

An ICU bed twisted at an angle next to a fallen IV tower. A signature of blood streaked the floor, and at the end of it, three MPs held a red-faced Yarrow on her stomach as she screamed. They weren't hurting her, but there was murder in her voice.

"Don't! Don't do it to me!"

"Wait!" I called to the MPs.

I ran, slipped on the blood, and fell, getting my wrist out of the way in time to land on my elbow. I scurried to her, getting on my knees. She'd been fine, just fine, a few hours ago. She'd been smiling and calm. Now she'd bitten her tongue and was bleeding out of her mouth.

"Ma'am," the MP said, "we have to move her out."

"Hang on. It's Doctor Frazier, Leslie. Can you see me?"

She looked at me. Or to be more accurate, her eyes landed in my direction.

I wanted to reach into her and pull out her pain. I wanted her to watch me wrestle it down and kill it for her. But it wasn't ever that easy. Ever.

"Don't," she pleaded. "Please."

"I won't hurt you."

"Don't let him do it to me again." She tried to get loose, but the MP held her more tightly.

I leveled my gaze at her. "You're sa—"

"Ma'am! Stand away."

"Don't let him hurt me!" Yarrow shouted. "Tell him

tomorrow." Tears ran across the bridge of her nose and mixed with the blood.

"Not today. Not tomorrow."

"If you talk nice to Daddy, he listens sometimes."

"He's dead, Leslie. He died alone and miserable."

She broke down in tears. The doc on staff swabbed her arm and gave her a sedative.

I turned my attention to the MPs. The one who had told me to get away was firm but not without compassion in his expression.

"Be gentle with her," I said. "Please."

"We will be."

Caden stood in the doorway with his arms crossed. I couldn't look at him. He was my strength and stability. I was a buoy in a storm, and he anchored me to the sea floor. But he'd gone through the same treatments as Yarrow and gotten a placebo for the same reason. Knowing he could turn into a screaming face on the hospital floor was too much to bear.

"YOU ALREADY SIGNED off on the shot." Dana articulated every word as if speaking more slowly would help me understand. She had her hands folded between her knees, and she sat on the edge of the chair on the other side of my desk. "If she left without it, the paperwork would be wrong."

"I am aware of that. Thank you. From now on, BiCam is not to be administered without me."

"So, I should have *knocked*?" Confrontation with a side of sarcasm, because of course, who knocks on a bedroom door when they can hear the bed squeaking? People have *shame*.

"Yes, you should have knocked."

Her eyes went just a little wider.

"Dana." I folded my hands on my desk. "People fuck. They do it behind closed doors, in beds that sometimes squeak."

"Awkward."

"Would you rather feel awkward or have an episode like that?"

"You don't know it was the shot. You said it was a placebo."

"I know."

"Was it a placebo or not?"

I tapped my fingertips together. The pamphlet said it was a placebo. The staff at Blackthorne NY had said it was placebo. It shouldn't have affected her at all.

Was it the breathing? Had I done it?

The door clicked open behind Dana, and Ferhad poked his head in. "New York is on in Conference Room Three."

———

"WE NEED THE SYRINGE," Ronin said from the screen.

"We have it," I said. I'd already stowed the syringe with its blue-tinted hub to send back.

"I need a report with every detail. The circular breaths. The shot. Everything." He leaned on the end of a long, shiny table with chairs around it. Through the windows on his right, New York was overlaid with late morning clouds. "That's not supposed to happen."

I leaned against the conference table in Baghdad with the same sun under the same sky in the windows. "Was it a placebo?"

"Yes. I'm sure."

"Are you sure there wasn't a mix-up?"

"We'll test it and let you know."

"I don't care what you test. What about Leslie? What are you going to do for her now?"

He shook his head slowly. Nothing he could do. Out of his hands. A woman had bitten her tongue bloody, but if it happened again, it was just because shit happened.

"I want you to test Caden's," I said. "Before I administer it, I want you to make sure it's a placebo."

"I can't unseal it." Putting his hands behind him, he grabbed the edge of the table. "That would defeat the purpose."

"How about I just don't give it to him?"

"I'll see if we can send a new one. How is that?"

"Fine."

"Fine. Moving on."

"Moving on," I agreed.

"You can't tie your PA's hands. She has to do her job."

"She didn't waste any time going to you, did she?"

"We only hire the best, Greyson. If the job needs to get done, it needs to get done. She doesn't need a babysitter."

Maybe I was being ridiculous. I had signed for the placebo because I thought it was fine. I would have given it to Yarrow even if Dana had knocked on the door. Blaming her was useless, and adding another layer of bureaucracy to our jobs wouldn't undo it. Prevention was in Dana seeing what had happened. She wouldn't want to be responsible for it happening again.

Chapter Seventeen

CADEN

Only the bottom ten feet of the Green Zone were actually green. High walls and barbed wire didn't keep out the rockets and mortars. I knew from personal experience that a suicide bomber could get past the gates and checkpoints.

The Green Zone was at least as dangerous as Balad Air Base had been three years before, yet it was different. Not more or less. Just different.

When I had been at Balad, Greyson was close to me. She was a major in the army. She was protected.

At Balad, I'd been sane.

Now, I wasn't.

I'd said a lot of things in New York when the whispers started, but I'd never let myself believe that I was truly insane. I'd admitted to a problem. A temporary illness. A set of symptoms curable with the right treatment.

But when I saw Yarrow crawling on the floor, overtaken by fears she thought she'd overcome, I called her insane in my mind. I had compassion for her plight, but at the same time, I categorized her neatly. She was crazy.

It was a dismissal, and I didn't realize I was doing it until I recognized the child's pleas that came out of her mouth. A woman's voice with a child's desperation. An identity twisted backward on itself.

What was the difference between her and me?

Nothing.

Nothing at all.

I came to this at my most lucid, right after tying my wife to the bed, but two days later, when the buzz started swarming, the reality of it had to be shut away. It had to be denied. I grabbed control, and the diligence it took to hold that control meant what it always did.

I had no feelings one way or the other about whether or not I was sane. I had a job to do. The Thing that buzzed and sometimes had a name sucked all the worry and fear into itself, leaving me in peace.

It was a great system even if it was crazy.

When the rockets fell after the midnight prayer, I got

dressed. The casualties got to the hospital as the second round shook the earth.

"That was close," the paramedic said, wheeling in an Iraqi civilian who'd had a wall fall on his arm. He stopped where I told him, and the nurse cut the man's sleeve open while I got his vitals.

"Where were you?" I asked as I checked him over.

"At my daughter's house in Kardat Maryam," he said in accented but excellent English.

I didn't have a good sense of where the neighborhoods began and ended, but that was close to Greyson's apartment. It was late. She'd be home.

The nurse opened the sleeve.

"This hurt?" I pressed a spot on his swelling forearm.

He nodded vigorously.

"X-ray," I said to the nurse. "This is Boner's." I turned back to the patient. "We're going to x-ray your arm, and an orthopedist is going to take a look at you."

"Yes. All right."

"Was the neighborhood hit badly?"

"The house is half off."

"And the buildings around it?"

I was sorry about his daughter's house, but I needed to

know if my wife was on her way into the ER or under a pile of rubble.

"Nothing. Like God was protecting them."

I DIDN'T BELIEVE in God without Greyson. Didn't buy his protection or his love. My faith only went as far as her well-being. It would snap back if anything happened to her.

I lay awake in the hours before dawn with the Green Zone quiet and my patients recovering. She was all right. She would have come through the doors if she'd been injured.

But the buzz didn't believe it. The buzz needed to check before it let me sleep. I was on medevac duty in three hours, where I'd sit in a room waiting for a nine-line that might never come. I'd stare down the black swarm. I'd keep it locked up while it pushed against its boundaries, forcing me to acknowledge its existence, while I tried to convince myself that I wasn't out of my fucking mind.

I was in my room, pacing. Pretending I had it under control. I wasn't panicked as much as I knew this wasn't right.

I tried to call her. The signal here was so bad calls dropped before they rang, and the one time I got through, my wife didn't pick up.

The shelling had stopped. I was off duty. If she was in danger, I'd know it by now. She would have been wheeled in.

And yet...

And yet...

You can't take care of her.

I froze.

The buzz didn't coalesce into Damon's voice. There wasn't a question in it. It wasn't immature and cowardly. The buzz growled its words. It was angry. I felt its rage like a knife in my thoughts, not a cloud over them.

What would it be to unleash this Thing?

I snapped up my jacket.

I RANG the bell outside her apartment. When she didn't answer, I took inventory of the wall. There were no streetlights, but the moon showed me no way to scale it. I pressed it again. If she didn't answer in sixty seconds, I'd check the perimeter. Maybe there would be a way to climb over in the back.

The light went from blue to yellow. Her light.

Voices. A woman and a man. The blade cut through my thoughts again.

"I don't know," she said.

Not Greyson. The blade retracted, but I was aware of its presence in the sheath.

The little window behind the gate opened, and a man's face looked through. "Who's there?"

"I'm looking for Greyson."

"That's Caden," the woman's voice said. "Her husband." It was Dana, chipper as always and, if I had to make a guess, a little tipsy.

The door snapped open. I recognized the man from a football game in Fallujah. With a hairline that had receded a few inches since the last time I saw him, he looked as if more than three years had passed.

"Pfc. Trona."

"Hey! Captain Fobbit." He held out his hand after Dana closed the gate behind me. "Oh, sorry. Major. Got your leaves, I see."

The front yard's hanging lights were on, and the little table had one plastic cup and a bottle of wine. Dana had the other cup in her hand.

"Yeah. I heard this neighborhood took some shelling."

"A little west of here."

"Everyone all right?"

He put his arm around Dana. "All good. I thought you went home."

"Didn't last."

"Greyson's upstairs," Dana said as my wife's door opened on the veranda above.

Greyson leaned over the railing in sweatpants and slippers, her back bathed in light from her apartment. The army T-shirt was worn to gauze, and she had to cross her hoodie over her hard nipples. "Caden?"

She hustled down, zipping her sweatshirt, and I went to the bottom of the stairs to meet her. "I wanted to make sure you were all right."

"I'm fine."

"Come sit," Trona said, "have some wine."

Dana reached under the table for the sleeve of cups. "Yeah! Hang out."

Neither Greyson nor I answered. I couldn't stop looking at her body. The brown eyes, warm in the chilly night, her feet in her slippers. The perfectly-shaped toes in front, a genetic gift, with the calluses from hard work in the back. Her hair was a nest from sleep, and her eyes were puffy. I didn't need to see the scar under her shirt or inside her right wrist to know they were there. This was what a woman looked like when she'd lived her life fully. The choices she made were all over her body and her manner.

"Sit, sit!" Dana said. "Was it busy at the hospital after the shelling? We didn't get a call that one of ours came in."

"Not too bad," I said with my eyes on my wife. I was so intent on her I didn't notice the buzz or concern myself with the angry voice.

Greyson sat on the bench and took a cup from Trona. She thanked him and, with a glance and a smirk, invited me to sit next to her. The night was quiet except for the wind and the crickets that dotted the white walls of the building. The buzz had been tamed for the moment. The woman I'd married was safe and beautiful.

"You knew these guys?" Dana asked Trona when we were all sitting. "Was it from Fallujah?"

"Yeah. Threw a football around with this guy."

"You have a good arm," I said. "Are you stationed here?"

"Contracting. Can't beat the money." He pointed his cup at the window next to Greyson's. "I live in the apartment right up there."

"Don't let him fool you," Greyson said with a smile. "He's been living in the apartment downstairs since he met this lady."

Trona put his arm around Dana, and they shared a kiss.

"At least when he's here," she said with a playful pout. "He's out doing security runs all the time."

"Fucking nuts out in the Red." He shook his head.

I let my hand creep over to Greyson's lap, sliding it over hers. We wove our fingers together.

"Tell me about it," I said.

"What are they calling you here?" Trona poured more wine. "Can't call you Fobbit anymore."

"Asshole Eyes," Greyson said with a scowl.

Trona cracked up. "I'm not even gonna ask."

"What's Fobbit?" Dana asked.

"It means he's an inexperienced rube who doesn't go over the wire," Greyson said, swirling her cup. "Which I preferred."

"Yeah," Trona said. "After that medevac you were on in Fallujah, I'm surprised you ever went out again. More power to you, man. I drink to your balls."

"What happened?" Dana asked.

"Nothing," I said. "Not that big a deal."

"We had sniper fire on a convoy out. He was good. Hit a full bird colonel."

"Colonel Brogue," Greyson said.

"Yeah, and civ haji were everywhere. Our guy hit a woman running away. I dragged her into the building we were holed up in, but she was bleeding bad out her leg."

"Femoral artery," I added. I didn't want him to recount

this story. Not here. Not ever. But I couldn't react, or I'd overreact. It was easier to tamp it all down. "It was a mess, but we got there in time."

"For the colonel," Trona added. "But that lady with her screaming? Gave away our location."

I was about to change the subject, but Greyson leaned forward as if she was interested in his story. I put my eyes on my cup. It was half-filled with blood.

"Then what?" Greyson prodded.

"We held them off. But the medic's trying to put on the tourniquet, and she's screaming his name, this guy right here." He indicated me. "Or I thought that was what it was. St. John. *Dujon, dujon.* Like, okay we get it. You want the doctor. Can we not tell the world where we are?"

"Oh, my God." Dana was rapt, and Trona loved it.

I tried to take a sip of wine, but the liquid in my cup smelled like copper and discarded tissue.

"We dragged her and the doc into a fucking closet while we waited for a pickup and tried to get things under control. When we opened it..." He paused.

Maybe he was checking my reaction. I didn't know. The cup was full, and it reeked of death.

"She was dead. The tourniquet held, but there was blood everywhere. Man."

Greyson's hand was cold in mine.

"Our interpreter said *dujon* wasn't the name on Fobbit's uniform," Trona said. "He told us in the chopper, didn't you hear? It means 'I'm pregnant.'"

"She miscarried from blood loss." Greyson's voice was an electric blanket that warmed the air and fried the mind at the same time. "And it killed her."

"Dunno," Trona said.

"That's right," I said flatly. "That's exactly what happened."

Greyson let go of my hand, and my world narrowed into a long, endless hallway.

"Oh, my God, no more war stories!" Dana cried. "Let's polish off this bottle. Okay?"

My wife swigged the last gulp of wine and put down her cup. "You guys finish it. I have to be up early tomorrow."

She got up and went to the steps. I knew that if I didn't follow right behind, she'd slam the door in my face.

I was right. At the top, she got it halfway closed. I put my hand on it and passed through.

"Get out," she hissed.

I shut the door behind me. "What's the problem?"

"You lied. You said she lived. You said everyone lived. You *lied* to me."

"So what?"

She turned toward her bedroom, and I knew I wasn't invited there.

"How does what happened that night affect you?" I asked. "Or us? Or anything?"

"You. Lied." Her voice was as steady and thick as the air around us.

"I had my reasons."

"Good night, Caden. Be safe walking back."

My wife could yell. She could get spitting, kicking, screaming mad. But this? She was stating facts with utter clarity, as if she'd looked at the situation from down the block and decided to cross the street to keep her distance from it.

No.

She never walked away from a conflict.

Anger swelled, stretched, heavy as a water balloon filled to the breaking point.

In two steps, I had her arm clasped in my fingers.

"Don't touch me."

The man I'd always been released her, but the buzzing rage heard the hard flatness in her voice and wouldn't let go.

Hurt her.

"It's nothing." I heard myself growl as if I was an observer.

Hurt her until she listens.

"Let me go, or your balls are going to be removed from your body."

The threat didn't move me. I wasn't worried about my testicles. But I made a calculated decision that I had nothing to gain from holding her, and the angry man inside me, the one who was pushing to get out, agreed with the assessment and released her arm.

"You can do anything to me," she said. "You can hurt me. You can push every boundary I have. But lying? Lying's a line, and you crossed it."

"I had to."

She cocked her head and folded her arms.

"I didn't want to talk about it."

"Not acceptable."

"You have no right to be this way. Whether or not a casualty died has no effect on you or us. It's none of your damn business."

She was going to try to redefine her business, and I was prepared to answer her point for point, then I was going to fuck the—

"How many times?" She interrupted my train of thought.

"How many times what?"

"You lied about the woman. You lied about the word *dujon...*"

"I just forgot it."

"You lied about your father."

Now I wanted to choke her. My hands flexed into fists and unflexed. She looked at them, then back at my face. Her fearlessness was a clinical condition.

"You pushed too far, Caden. Multiple times. Over years. Lies of omission. Lies of minimization. Lies I don't even know about. And I let you get away with it. I pretended you hadn't gone over the line, but I knew. I knew."

"What's the fight for, *baby*?" Baby wasn't a coo; it was a gunshot, and I was too deep inside anger to mitigate the damage. "You want to sit here all night and grill me about every word I've ever said to you? What's your endgame? You want to split up? Walk away? If I crossed some kind of line with you, let's talk about how you react when I tell you things. Because you're pushy. You're stubborn. You don't do what you're fucking told, and you have no regard for me as a separate person. I only exist as I relate to you."

Anger is always a partner to righteousness, and I was fucking right. She was an impossible woman to deal with. A life-sucker. A divorce waiting to happen. Standing there looking at the floor between us, as still as a predator waiting for an opening. Not to kill me. No, an opening to love me to fucking death.

And yet... I wanted her, and I wanted her to want me. And I wanted her to move the damned line for the lies the way she moved it for everything else.

And yet... what I wanted was taking a back seat to something much more toxic.

"What?" I leaned toward her. "Nothing to say? Not spouting all the answers? For once?"

That lit a fire under her. "Go home."

Her anger opened a gate wide, releasing a swarm of hornets. I had to look away so she didn't see the full-throated rage, and when I did, I saw a paper rectangle on the table.

A sonogram. Early. Under twelve weeks.

It took a split second to analyze it.

I didn't know what I looked like when I turned back to her, but I was covered in darkness and the buzz, the leash broken, unable to pull back the need to break her.

It took her a single move to get past the threshold to her room. She slammed the door before I could reach her, and the bang of wood hitting wood made the earth shake and tilt.

Chapter Eighteen

GREYSON

At first, I thought he was banging on the door. I thought he was banging so hard the ground shook. I thought he hit the door forcefully enough to shake the plaster from the walls and ceiling with a deep, ear-splitting *pow*. He must have grown twenty feet tall, bursting through the upper story and the roof. His rage was an explosion of rock and a rain of dust.

I crouched, arms over my head to protect me from his falling debris. It didn't work. I was knocked over by it. It filled my lungs with fire and smothered me in darkness.

GREYSON, Greyson, Greyson—baby, baby, baby—I want to tell you a story.

HIS VOICE CIRCLED the outer reaches of my consciousness. There was blood and black, air thick in my nose and hot in my lungs. A driving cramp in my gut and a sharp ache in my head. I couldn't move. I thought my eyes were closed, then I blinked. It was so dark I couldn't tell the difference. I coughed, and a warm flood soaked my pants.

What a time to get my period.

"Greyson?"

His voice. A bark. Close. Five feet? Three?

"Caden." I was alive. "Where are you?"

"Right here." His voice seemed deeper in the small space. A low roar. "Can you move?"

I took stock of my extremities. "My arms. There's something heavy on my legs."

Glass clinked as he moved toward me. "Can you feel them?"

I felt him near, but there was no light. I couldn't see, and my head hurt too much to move. "They hurt."

"That's good." He swallowed the last word into a rasp. A growl from deep in his chest. His hand fell on my hair splayed over the floor, gripping and pulling.

He released my hair, and our hands found each other in the darkness. He squeezed my fingers so hard he hurt me, and I became deeply aware of the small space and my inability to move inside it.

"Caden? Are you crying?"

No. This wasn't crying. He was hurtling air out of himself. This was something deeper. An inner battle I couldn't fathom.

He uttered a single word. It was rage and danger in a syllable, barked like an animal in a cage.

"No."

Chapter Nineteen

CADEN

The brain craves information. It starves in the absence of light. Pupils dilate like open mouths, crowding the irises until they're thin rings of color. That's all eyes are—collectors of information for a brain wired to make sense of the environment with very little data.

Modern people rarely experience complete darkness. Light pollution smothers out the darkness. Even without it, starlight can illuminate the path ahead. A sliver of moon behind clouds sends enough data to the brain to make out shapes.

When there's nothing, like in a cave or a windowless concrete cellar, the other senses collect more information, cracking open perceptions that are usually shut.

The smack of the mortar shell came at the same moment she slammed the door in my face, and the ensuing heat, fire, and rumble came as I cracked inside, letting the anger take shape, fully formed.

It had a name, but I wouldn't say it, and getting knocked over by half a wall took the wind out of its appearance. It was half in, half out, like a dog stuck in the cat door.

In the distance, more shells fell. I had to breathe. Take stock. The rubble had formed a pocket of complete darkness. A drop of warm liquid fell over my cheek. I was cut. My hands were free. I touched my face. Glass. I removed what I could. My foot was under something heavy. I shifted it, and a brick came off easily, but when I tried to turn, glass clinked under me, and a sharp pain seared the heel of my hand.

"Greyson?"

She didn't answer. The wall between us must have crumbled, because her breathing was close. I pulled my sleeves over my hands and crawled to her. My back scraped against something hard. Tight space. Dark. I felt for her body. She was so close. I could smell her. Hear her. I could sense the blood pulsing through her body, but I couldn't find her.

If she was dead, the Thing would eat me alive in fury.

"Baby. Please."

Rock. Just rock. Such a small space and such infinite darkness.

A woman I loved in such danger, in such a tight space, and me—helpless to save her.

This wasn't—

This didn't—

No. I was a grown man.

I wasn't—

I didn't—

"Greyson."

The smell of blood everywhere. She had to be all right. This couldn't happen. Not again. Not to me. The blood was copper and broken bodies. It flowed like a river, and it was my fault. The anger with the name I wouldn't articulate wedged its way out another inch, growling and hissing simultaneously.

No.

"Greyson!"

Her name was a shout in the dark, eaten by a small space without an echo. I didn't hear a response, but my hearing had been sharpened on the stone of darkness. I would have sworn I heard her heart beating. Maybe it was my own heart. Maybe they were beating with matching rhythms.

I wouldn't give up on her. Not now. Not ever. I wouldn't lose anything else in the dark. I'd lost too many women in the dark. Too many had hurt in my hands but out of my sight.

Not Greyson. Never Greyson.

I took a deep breath so I could call louder, harder. Bring her back from the dead if I had to. The air cracked into dust and shards, slicing my windpipe on the way down. I coughed before I could scream her name again.

"Caden." She was alive. "Where are you?"

Her voice. The sound of an angel choking on sand and broken seashells.

I reached for it and found a handful of her hair. I left myself. I was in a closet. I was in the bottle room. I was trapped in the smell of blood and hopelessness.

"Right here. Can you move?" My voice was swallowed by the air, pressed into impotence. Anger, unreasonable and explosive, pushed against judgment. It howled a single word with both insult and justification.

Dujon.

"I don't know," Greyson said. "Where are you?"

Her voice pulled me to reason.

I hadn't realized how dead still the air was until it moved from the swing of her arms. I found her hand, and the touch wasn't fortifying. It split the membrane, hitting me like a bomb on an apartment building.

Dujon.

"Can you move?" I asked, focusing on the moment, not the crowd of memories funneling into my consciousness.

She's pregnant.

She's pregnant.

"My arms. There's something heavy on my legs."

I'm trying to understand her, but nothing makes sense.

Her legs. My wife's beautiful legs.

Covered in so much blood, I thought she was wearing stockings.

"Can you feel them?" I was on my belly near her, squeezing her hand. I felt her pulse on my fingers, but the buzz was too loud. I couldn't count.

I blamed the darkness. I blamed my weakness.

"They hurt."

"That's good."

"Caden. Are you crying?"

"No."

I spit the word in a voice of pure instinct and raw fury. Maybe I was crying, but it wasn't sadness. Oh, no. It was something more powerful and far less manageable. It didn't have words. Just sounds meant to scare prey into shocked stillness. I was fighting a monster's release, pushing against two sets of events I wanted to forget while my most recent lucid memory was the love of my life slamming a door in my face.

I reached for her and was greeted with a hard, flat surface. Not stone. Wood.

"It's the door," she said. "I think it fell on me, and something's holding it down."

A door between us.

Not a wall.

Dujon, dujon

"I'm all right," she said as if she could feel my panic. "Someone will come."

Why is she saying my name over and over in the dark?

"If I change, Greyson baby, you have to leave me."

"What?!" Her alarm echoed in the space, bringing the realization of how small it was.

My heart rate picked up in panic, and my defenses weakened further. The swarm of hornets buzzed, pushing against the force of my will.

"Never see me again."

It's not your fault, sweetheart. It's just—

That slammed door. Her pushed in. The slap of the lock.

"What's happening?" she asked from far, far away.

"Promise me!" I demanded. "Promise *now*."

"No!"

Our hands found each other. I felt for the hard circle of her ring.

—you're going to have a little sister.

But I wasn't. Not after the lock of the door.

"Mmm," I said, barely audible to myself. I sounded like my own hallucination.

"Never."

It wasn't just the darkness; it was the thickness of it. The weight. The way it closed in while the sounds outside kept on and on like life moving without me.

And the smell. Cloying and coppery. Slurred words and panic swirling into a whirlwind.

"It was my fault."

"Caden?"

Caden?

Dr. John.

She squeezed my hand, and I was boy and man. Adult and child. I could make choices, and I was trapped in my impotence. Cut loose from her and twined with her forever.

"What's happening, Caden? Talk to me."

She needed me.

She needs me because...

"I knew she was pregnant."

"The Iraqi woman?" Greyson said in the darkness. "In Fallujah?"

"I had no idea she was pregnant."

Both were true. I lived two separate realities concurrently. The Iraqi woman spoke with my mother's voice in the darkness.

Dujon.

"She was bleeding," I said. "It was everywhere. She was dying. Because of me. Because I got a B on my history essay. It was the punctuation. The commas. He cut off her air to show me the difference between a *pause* and a *stop*, and when I ran downstairs..."

Boy, you're a coward.

"He put her in there with me. Bullet right through the thigh. The medic tied off the femoral artery, but her pressure dropped and her body got rid of the baby to save itself. I was scared he'd come down and see the mess and hurt her again."

I heard Greyson's response but didn't understand the words. I heard only strength and comfort, as if she was a guide through a frightening and alien land. She pulled me forward.

"She let him do it." I wasn't sure if I was speaking out loud or if the clay-thick air absorbed the sound before anyone heard. "Why did she let him? What the hell was wrong with her? Fuck her. Fuck her for letting him hurt her. God. There's so much blood. She's not moving. She's limp. Her arms and legs. She's—"

—*dead. My mother is dead, and I killed her with a B in history because I wasn't careful.*

—*dead. This woman is dead because you didn't listen to her.*

My wife was saying something. The syllables ran together to make one word said in my mother's voice, in a dark closet with gunfire on the other side of the wall and the smell of blood all over the cellar and my eleven-year-old hand being squeezed into pain.

Dujon.

Losing blood.

Duyon.

Blood pressure dropping.

Dayon.

Words slurring.

Danyon.

Heart stopping.

Damon.

The anger breached the crack, and its name became a hard buzz, drowning out the soft-bellied Damon. I was busting from the inside, swelling into a third person of unlimited, ever-expanding rage.

I articulated his name. It was no more or less than a roar without cadence or syllables. Unspellable, unspeakable, a sound that shook the earth and made the broken man inside me shrink into a pin dot.

The bag closed, only this time it wasn't a soft bag held with string, but a tiny room with a metal door. Black as night, I was alone again, listening to the sounds from the kitchen above as he tormented her for all the things I'd done wrong.

"Caden!"

I was so small. Four years old with fat little hands against the cold, concrete wall and the taste of stolen birthday cake on my tongue.

"Caden, listen to me." Greyson's voice from the kitchen. She was getting beaten up there, and she was calling me. "Fight it. Fight hard. I love you. I'm waiting for you. Push against it. You're bigger than this."

I couldn't feel my body. Every sense was muffled, but still she called me.

"I need you. Please. I need you. This is not your limit. You're bigger than this limit. Find it. Find who you are. Breathe. Breathe for me."

What was it about her voice that cut through the sound in my ears and the thick walls around me? She was so calm even as I was hurting her in the kitchen.

"Listen," she whispered, and I heard it. "*Soo-hoo. Soo-hoo.* Breathe with me."

The angry thing believed in destruction. The angry thing roared and growled. It didn't believe in bullshit meditative breathing. But my lungs did, and they obeyed, dragging the dense air in and out without a pause. Dizzying, confusing the angry thing taking me over, while the child in the basement felt the walls go soft.

Soo-hoo. Soo-hoo.

And Damon returned from a deep, deep sleep with his basket of needs and insecurities.

The buzz turned on him.

Soo-hoo. Soo-hoo.

You're weak.

You're worthless.

You're broken.

You are a blemish.

"Caden." Her voice was the pin of gravity, the edges of the Universe, and the anchor holding me to the center of it.

But I couldn't respond to her. It was too much. I was still

breathing with a rhythm, even without her guidance, as Damon swirled into the same space as the anger.

I pitied him. I wanted to protect him. But he didn't need my protection. He was ready to die.

"Caden," she repeated without doubt or weakness. "Go into it. Don't run away. Embrace it. This is you. They're all you. I love you."

She was here, in the darkness—

Soo-hoo. Soo-hoo.

—with every mistake I ever made and—

Soo-hoo. Soo-hoo.

—she still loved me.

All the doors opened. A single space in my mind where blame and guilt and cowardice lived next to honesty and bravery and love.

I became aware of my body again, and in one gulped breath, I was whole.

Part Three

SHATTERING

Chapter Twenty

GREYSON

I had a concussion from a falling wooden beam. Boner confirmed the door had saved my leg. It had cracked and fallen on me first, then distributed the impact force of the concrete piece that fell on it. I had a "dead leg," a quadricep contusion that looked as if I'd spilled black and red paint on my thigh just above the knee.

It hurt like hell, truth be told. The pain didn't bother me because my mind was completely occupied with Caden.

Under the rubble of my apartment building, I'd talked him through something neither of us had understood at the time. At one point, he'd just rested his head on my chest, and I'd stroked his hair. We'd waited in silence until we heard the trucks outside, then we shouted for all we were worth. As the voices of rescuers got closer, our shouts were mixed with relieved laughter. When the first shaft of light shot through the debris, I saw him for the first time since I'd slammed the door in his face.

"Wow," was all I could say. He was covered in a mask of gray dust, but the blue of his eyes reflected the morning light like windows to the sky, just like they always did, except for one thing.

The sky wasn't frightening. It was clear and calm, a protective shield not just over me, but over him as well.

"You look stunning yourself," he'd said from above me. "Not that you have a choice, but stay still."

Then he'd looked at the rescue team as they moved another slab, getting between me and the pebbles falling from the sky.

IF I'D STILL HAD my commission, they'd have sent me to Germany to recover, then decide if I had to go back to my unit or go home. But I was a contractor and part of the conversation about my own best interests. The military hospital kept me overnight to monitor the concussion.

In the dim light, surrounded by the soft hiss of machines, Caden leaned into my bed. "Dana and Trona are fine. Minor contusions. A few scrapes. They got sent home."

A rectangle of bandage clung to his forehead where he'd been cut by falling glass.

"For scrapes?"

"Home, Baghdad home."

"It's a pile of rock."

"Blackthorne owns a third of the Green Zone." He sat next to the bed and stroked my cheek. He wasn't the cold, detached man we'd fought to control, nor did he have the soft, insecure expression I'd come to know as Damon's. He was neither and both. He was impossibly complete.

"What's different about you?" I asked.

"Everything." Even his voice was somehow more whole, like a puzzle with all the pieces in place. "It's over."

"It can't be," I said. "Nothing's that easy."

"You call that easy?"

"I don't even know what it was."

"It was all the stuff I never told you." He slid his hand under mine and laid the other one on top. "I'm sorry, Greyson. I'm so sorry I lied to you. I thought if I relived it, I'd... I don't know. Die, maybe, if I want to overstate it." He brushed his thumb along the side of my hand with that perfect pressure I'd come to love. "Let me tell you what happened twice. No, two and a half times."

He was quiet for a long time.

"I wasn't afraid of the dark when I was a kid," he said. "I wasn't afraid of anything. I was like you."

"I'm afraid of plenty."

He shrugged as if I was splitting hairs. "If you say so."

"I'm sorry I interrupted. Go on."

After a short pause, he began again. "I went in the bottle room when I was scared. I could hear everything from the floor above, but I felt safe. I told you this, but I didn't tell you the last time I went down there. I was about eleven. I wasn't a careful kid. I didn't cross my Ts and or dot my Is generally, and composition wasn't my strong subject. I'd gotten back a history essay with too many corrections. Commas. Fucking commas."

I nodded. "Commas are sneaky."

He smiled in the dim light. "I was in a gifted school, and there was a lot of homework. I was tired when I wrote the essay, and I didn't check it over. He—my father—took it out on my mother. Sometimes I got mad at her for putting up with it, but I was always more mad at myself for not checking my work. Like she knew it, she always made sure to blame herself. The more I think about it, the more I think that was why I fell in love with you." He looked at me and squeezed my hand. "You'd never put up with that from me."

I held back a comment, but he read my mind.

"Except on your terms," he said with half a grin. "That's safe for me. Until it wasn't. Then... you know what happened."

"Damon."

"I protected myself from hurting you. I was already

fucked in the head with him pushing on me because he was my protector."

"Did you feel split before then though?"

"No, I don't know what opened that up."

I had a feeling I knew what it was, but I wasn't ready to admit my hand in his breakdown. Not to him and not to myself. But I knew.

"Here's what I never told you." He cleared his throat and looked away. "That time, with the commas, he put her in the bottle room with me and locked the door from the outside. He did that sometimes with just me but not for long. This time, after the history essay, it was different. Jesus, this is hard."

I let it be hard. He hadn't dealt with any of it. Hadn't looked it in the face and taken control of it.

"I could hear her, but I couldn't see her. She was crying. She didn't cry in front of me. But she was across that little room, sobbing. And I was on the other side, feeling like it was all my fault but also resenting her for invading my safe place. Then she was groaning in pain. And I said, 'Mom, are you all right?' and she said, 'It's your sister.'"

He didn't have a sister.

"And that..." he said with a deep breath from the bottom of his lungs. "That was when I smelled the blood." His face scrunched into a knot, revealing every beautiful dimple. "It was sticky. So sticky and thick. The smell...

and there was so much. Just on and on. A puddle. I thought she was dying. I thought..." Another deep breath he had trouble taking. "I thought I'd killed her."

"She was miscarrying," I whispered, and he nodded.

"I didn't know that. I couldn't see her, and she kept saying she was fine. I thought he'd stabbed her over commas. My commas."

"It wasn't your fault."

He pressed my hand to his lips and closed his eyes. "I didn't know what to do." His lips moved against my knuckles. "She just lay there and said it was okay. She said it wasn't my fault. She forgave me."

"Do you forgive her?"

"Not really. When she stopped groaning from the cramps, I crawled over to her. I got blood all over my hands and knees. She didn't move. I picked up her arm, and it was like a dead weight." He rested his head on my belly, the bandage disappearing in the folds of the sheets, looking at me with sideways eyes. "I swore to her that when we got out, I'd never miss another thing. I'd pay attention to every detail no matter how tired I was. She said, 'Okay.' That was how I knew she wasn't dead."

I ran my fingers through his hair. I was mad at Caden's father for being too dead to face justice, but I wasn't mad at Caden for lying. Not anymore. All the boundaries between us were false walls.

"And then," he continued. "The woman in the closet. The femoral artery. It was like I was eleven again. I asked her to forgive me, but she didn't understand my shitty Arabic."

"Because she was Kurdish."

"I think that was when I first felt Damon, but he was so small."

"And you were doing surgery all the time. The army too. So orderly it was safe to keep him in the background."

His eyes were transparent in the cold light of the moon. "In the rubble, it was different. No Damon. Just a monster. I swear, if you hadn't talked me through it, I don't know what I'd be now. I can do anything with you. I'm still fucked in the head, but it feels normal. I'm a fucked-up person but a *whole* fucked-up person. All the doors opened, and it's one room again."

"I think we stumbled on something," I said. "The breathing, plus the opportunity to face fear and get control. Maybe. I don't know. All I know is you look like the man I fell in love with before all this. You're the fucked-up, brave, honorable, strong asshole I love."

"I'm going to be everything you need from now on."

I believed him. I wasn't sure the world would let us be happy, but I was sure that if happiness was to be found, it was with him. All of him.

He sat up straight and got something from his pocket. He held it close before showing me.

Grady's sonogram.

"I understand why you didn't tell me," he said.

I laughed. He looked wounded.

"It's not mine."

"You lost it. I know." He took my hand as if I needed comfort, but he was the one who needed his hand held.

"No. No, no, no. It's from a soldier in Balad. He died, and I keep it for... I don't know why. Luck or respect."

He laughed once, softly, and the last of his tension fell off in a single breath. "Like a rabbit's foot." He plucked it off the bed.

"I would have told you," I said.

"I found it when we were fighting, so everything was upside down."

"Keep it for good luck or respect."

He slid it into his pocket and tilted his head right, then left to stretch his neck. "I have to get to work. I'll be in the next room if you need me."

"I need you. Trust me."

He bent to kiss my cheek, letting his lips linger on my skin. I turned, laying my mouth against his. Slowly, we entered into a kiss, savoring the taste and touch as if it were the first. His tongue gently met mine, and I melted into a pool of desire. With a leisurely pace, he opened his mouth, and I made my shape match his until we were bound by breaths and moans.

We jerked apart with a rustling of paper and the scrape of a chair behind him.

"I should go." He drew his thumb along my cheek. The corner of the bandage on his forehead had curled a little from laying his head on my chest, and I was struck again by the wholeness I'd taken for granted when we met and that I hadn't seen in a long time.

The Universe, assuming it even existed with a capital U, had a way of demanding Caden's attention. If there was any other explanation for his being repeatedly in dark rooms with bleeding women, I couldn't come up with it.

"We're very lucky," I said.

"There's someone up there watching out for us."

He was more prone to name divine causation than I ever thought possible.

You never really know a person.

Chapter Twenty-One

GREYSON

They let me out of the hospital the next day. I bought a set of crutches and got a lift to my new apartment. The building was much bigger. Thirty units opening onto shared balconies around a barren courtyard. All Blackthorne personnel. Fortified with a thick wall and barbed wire that wouldn't keep out a bomb any better than the last place.

I was in a single-room studio on the second floor.

"I'm on three," Dana said, unpacking the stuff she'd managed to retrieve from the rubble. "It's a longer walk up the stairs, but it's so great."

I was sure it would be "so great" no matter where she was.

RONIN WAS at my desk like he owned the place. He had a stack of files at one elbow and a cup of coffee at the other.

"Make yourself at home," I said, putting my crutches by the door. I didn't need them to walk but to keep the pressure off a leg working to heal.

"Thanks. I got you coffee." He flipped his hand to a cup by the guest chair. "Black, right?"

I picked it up. "You didn't say you were coming."

"Last minute." He flipped a page.

"What are you looking at?"

"Leslie Yarrow."

"How's she doing?"

"No clue." He closed the file and tossed it across the desk in my direction. "Do you have something useful to add to this fucking shitshow?" He leaned back with his hands linked over his diaphragm. "Because it wasn't supposed to turn out that way. I mean, maybe she's fine now, but that's not an excuse."

I flipped through the file. My report was on top. "I think you need to hold off on this program until you know."

He got pensive on me instead of addressing my suggestion. "Every treatment addressing PTSD focuses on reducing the trauma's impact by serving the trauma back with a sense of control. Facing fears. Defusing memories."

Behind my report was her circular breathing treatment schedule, the BiCam145 dosages, and her questionnaires.

"It's got to be done with a teaspoon," I said. "Not a shovel."

"Is that why you didn't give St. John his syringe?"

Calling my husband by his last name was a way to detach himself and me from the decision. A cute way to remind me that I was a clinician.

"No signs of trauma. He looked better on the way out than the way in."

"Unlike Linderman," he said.

"Unlike Yarrow."

"I feel *bad*." He drew out the last word as if remorse was a foreign concept.

"Like I said, I think you should suspend the program." I got to her application to enter the treatment. Scanned it. "Unless you like feeling *bad*."

"The upside's bigger than my feelings. Speaking of, how do you feel? Heard you were trapped for hours."

"It sucked. However—" I was going to tell him about Caden and facing fears. Defusing memory. Giving control. I was deciding what was Ronin's business, what would be helpful to the program and thus everyone, and what was too private to share. But I got to the last part of Yarrow's file and stopped on a card paper-clipped to a report copied from *Stars and Stripes*. I'd seen her file before but missed this. Leslie Yarrow's unit had been on the front lines in the second battle of Fallujah.

"However, being stuck with Caden St. John was tedious?" he said, trying to get under my skin and failing.

I read while Ronin jabbed me about my husband.

Yarrow's unit had been under sniper fire for three days. Surrounded. Trapped in an abandoned orphanage. They were getting picked off one by one until they rallied and made a heroic escape.

"Are you okay?" Ronin asked.

A single orange card was clipped to the sheet. A form filled in with stubby pencil. A date in 2003, a dosage, and all her basic info scrawled as if in a hurry.

"When you were with Intelligence," I asked, "did they have people embedded on the front lines?"

He shrugged. "Defense? Sure. Are you supposed to be standing with that leg?"

"I have two legs." I handed him the sheet and leaned on my good leg. "This is before you came to Balad."

"Yeah." He scanned the pages and handed them back to me.

"When we were at Balad, I had two jobs, more or less—evaluate soldiers for PTSD and keep the surgeons on their feet. I came with caffeine shots, vitamins, and amphetamine."

He leaned back again, pushing away from the desk. "You saved lives with those shots."

"You came with a synthetic amphetamine."

"I'll repeat—those shots saved lives."

"And according to this"—I held up the orange card —"Leslie Yarrow got it, probably with the rest of her unit. Helped with knowing if you were being watched, right? It heightens sensory cues, which wakes up the mind for a surgeon. But if you're being watched by, say, a sniper? You'd know where they were and when they saw you. It was a cure for scopaesthesia. Unless your paranoid fantasies are real."

"And thanks to it, they found a way out of an impossible situation. The same way it kept Caden and two other surgeons working in Balad."

I sat. Leaned forward. Folded my hands together on the desk. "I don't believe you."

Mirroring me, he leaned forward and folded his hands together on the desk. "I don't care."

"How many others who got that shot are presenting with dissociative disorder?"

"None who told the truth."

Well. There you had it. He knew. Maybe too late, but he knew. I should have been surprised, but I wasn't. I was, in a way, relieved.

"Why didn't you tell me you were looking at the questionnaires?"

"You weren't supposed to know. You would have asked questions, and I didn't want to answer questions." He sighed and put his hands flat on the blotter, looking out the window. "My whole career is defined by what I can and can't say to whomever I'm talking to. There are a lot of things I've wanted to tell you. That was why I wanted to bring you into intelligence. One of the reasons. There were more. And don't look at me like that. This isn't about you or friendship. It's not about our past together. It's about keeping our eyes on the prize. Those dumbasses in Abu Ghraib threw a once-in-a-lifetime opportunity out the window. They went from making Iraqi prisoners uncomfortable, which was the idea—you know, just have a woman look them in the eye or tell them what to do—and they went right to torture. Right to forcing them to suck each other off. It was disgusting. We could have won this war in half the time with half the deaths, but no. They didn't stay in the lines, and now here we are with a private company picking up where the US government had to stop."

My face was covered by my hands. I pressed my eyelids down until I saw exploding stars.

"I'm sorry, Greyson," he said. "It's for the greater good."

I wouldn't be able to talk him out of his ideals, no matter how misguided.

I took my hands off my eyes. "Is there anything else I should know?"

"You should know you're doing good work. Worthy work. Don't just look at what's gone wrong. Linderman is doing fine still. You know, from what you've seen, there's no way a guy in that serious a mental state is restored like that." He snapped his fingers. "Until now. We have to understand what happened with Leslie Yarrow and make adjustments. She won't be the last one."

The way he lowered his chin and dropped his voice a touch? He meant Caden.

I'D GIVEN Caden the code to my apartment. When I got back, he was already there, sitting by the light of a single lamp. He got up and greeted me without a word, only a deep kiss that tasted like musk and lust with the feel of a day's beard growth at the boundaries.

I pulled away to breathe, and he moved his attention to my cheek and neck.

"I have a few hours," he said.

"Lucky us. So do I."

Right at the door, he crouched and unlaced my boots. I stepped out of them. Kneeling, he undid my belt and fly. I unbuttoned my shirt.

"I've been thinking about you all day. What it will be like fucking you with everything intact. Just to fuck. Just to be there with you completely." He pressed his lips to my belly, sliding my pants down. "All of me."

Running his hands up and down my bare legs, he kissed every inch of skin he could find. I threaded my fingers in his hair.

All of him.

When was the last time we'd made love as a whole couple? Before his sensitivity took leave of his personality? Before his rage became a new threat? When was the last time the man I loved took me to bed?

A fear nagged.

Damon wasn't able to hurt me, and Damon was a part of him.

We'd discovered things about each other in the split. Would he be able to give me the same satisfaction? Would I be able to live without it?

"Caden," I said softly.

He stood, pushing me back against the door with kisses.

"Talk to me," he said, pressing the shape of his erection against me.

"I don't want you to do anything that doesn't feel right anymore." I put my nose to his and caressed his cheeks. He fit just right in my hands. "I'm not going to push you."

"That's fine," he said, taking my leg and draping it over his waist. "But I might push you."

My face stretched into a smile. I shouldn't have been that happy. He'd said he *might* push me. Meaning he might not be able to. But it was on the table, and that was good enough for me.

Pushing against me with the full force of his hips, he put my other leg around him and carried me to the bedroom.

Through a crack in the curtains, the room was cast in moonlight from the clear navy sky. He sat me on the edge of the bed. When he stood straight, I laid my hands on the bulge in his pants.

Our eyes met. Me below in nothing but my bra and underwear. Him above, fully dressed. In that look, we acknowledged his dominance and his power to choose whether or not to use it.

He laid his hand on my head and slid it to the side in a caress.

Maybe this was it. Maybe he would be a passionate and considerate lover for the rest of our lives. Maybe I would be blessed with a life of wonderful sex without bruising or pain. I tilted my head to nuzzle his arm because he had to choose and he needed to know that whatever choice he made didn't affect my love.

Before I turned my head completely, he gripped the hair at the base of my neck, pulling enough to control but not enough to hurt.

"It's not going to suck itself," he said.

A flood was unleashed between my legs.

With his hand still in my hair, he allowed me to undo his pants and get his cock out. It was rock hard, glistening at the tip. I licked off the salty precum.

"Don't be shy," he said. "Open your mouth."

He was everything. The dominant command of his voice. The control of his hand in my hair. My body raged for him.

I took him in my mouth, tasting the singular musk of his cock. I flattened my tongue and opened my throat. In three thrusts, I had his balls on my lower lip, and he yanked out so I could breathe. I looked up at him. His face was cast in shadow. The moonlight caught the square edge of his jaw.

"Again," he growled, pushing forward.

I took him for two thrusts, and on the third, he paused deep, pushing my face against his belly before yanking out. He wiped his spit-covered dick over my chin and lips.

This wasn't a blowjob. I wasn't sucking him to orgasm. This was him exerting control over me, my body, my will. This was a part of him brought out in the split, and it looked like it was here to stay.

I smiled and gave him a single word. "Yes."

He fucked my mouth one more time, then pulled out with a gasp. He was close. "Get on your back. Let's do this."

God, yes.

I flopped back in my underwear. Still fully dressed except for his slick, spit-wet dick, he pulled my knees up and apart. A thin, damp swatch of fabric separated my pussy from his eyes.

"What do you think I should do with you?" he asked with a tone that was less a question and more a command. Sitting on the edge of the bed, he stroked the crotch of my panties with the back of his hand.

"Whatever you want." I could barely answer with his hand brushing the fabric.

"Is this your way of not pressuring me?"

"Yes."

He slapped my pussy gently. My underwear diffused the sting into pure pleasure.

"Then you didn't answer my question." He tapped again, a little harder. "What should I do with you?"

He seemed so comfortable in his dominant role that I could have begged for anything, but through the intensity of my arousal, I still had doubts that he was capable of taking me the way Cold Caden had. I didn't want him to push himself so hard he regretted it. I needed a consent so clear its echoes would be felt in ten years.

"Whatever you want," I said.

"You are stubborn." He tapped hard, and it stung before turning into pleasure.

"I'm yours," I groaned. "It's up to you."

The next tap was a slap. It hurt. The pain was tenacious, and I twisted away. He held me down, pulling my legs apart again. He drew his fingernail over the fabric covering my clit, triggering every nerve ending.

"When I tell you to ask for something," he said, closing my legs, "I want you to ask for it."

He reached around my waist and pulled my underwear off before opening my legs again. My cunt was bare to him. There was no fabric to diffuse the pain now.

He slid two fingers inside me. I pushed toward him as if he were magnetized, keening toward the familiar unknown.

"I can do this until I have to show up at the hospital... or until you answer me." Pulling out, he flicked my clit.

I wanted to come so badly I thought desire would break me.

"What do you want?" he asked.

"My body is your toy."

The slap came fast and hard, and the sting was unmitigated, bursting into exquisite pain before it blossomed into excruciating pleasure. He held me down by holding my legs apart at the knees.

"Say it," he said. "I want you to say it."

His head was tilted toward the window, and in the moonlight, I saw the completeness of his power. The sexual command was part of a whole man.

He needed consent as much as I did.

"I want..." Breathless, I collected my thoughts. "I want it to hurt the most when it feels the best. I want to come with pain."

Watching his face for reticence, I saw only satisfaction.

"Use your teeth," I said. "Your hands. Your belt. Break me. Please."

He took his hands off me, letting my knees drop. I had half a second to worry before he spoke. "Good. Turn over onto your stomach."

When I did, he laid his hands on my hips and pulled them up.

"Get your knees under you. Put your ass up."

Behind me, I heard him undressing. I looked back.

"Turn around."

His grace was apparent in his shadow moving against the opposite wall. Shirt. Undershirt. Pants. He took his sweet time. I'd never wanted to fuck a shadow before.

The bed tilted when he put his knee on it.

When I saw the shadow twist, I thought he was going to fuck me. Instead, a slap and a burn landed on my ass. I gasped.

"Shh, baby. Keep it down."

"Okay."

"This may sting a little at first."

He slapped me again.

And again.

He slapped my ass until he had to shake out his hand. Until I was raw and tears streamed down my face. He caressed the skin and slapped again. He hit me until it burned even when he wasn't touching me.

"This is so hot," he said, running his hands over my sore skin. "So fucking hot."

He cruelly drove four fingers along the length of my

seam, and yet I came with that single touch, exploding involuntarily with a cry I had to choke back.

He knew I'd come. He had to, but he didn't mention it. He slapped my ass again. It wasn't hard, but it hurt.

"Open up. Show me what you have."

Laying my cheek on the bed, I reached back to my raw ass and gingerly touched it, sucking in air from the searing pain. I braced myself and grabbed it, pulling the cheeks apart so he could see.

The bed shifted. His shadow got taller as he kneeled between my legs and ran the head of his cock along me. "Open wider."

He could get in. I knew that. But he wanted me to touch that reddened skin so I could hurt like I'd begged to be hurt.

"Nice, baby. That's nice."

I was so wet he got his dick in me to the root with no resistance, pushing deep against my sore bottom. Moving out slowly.

"Is this what you wanted?"

"Yes."

He slammed into me. "I love fucking you. I love hurting you." Bending down, he put his weight on my back, flattening me as he fucked me. "I love being inside your sweet little cunt. Your tight ass. I love seeing my cock in your face."

My ass was on fire with every thrust. Had he left me any skin? Or had he seared it all off to break me?

"You're beautiful when you cry," he said. "When the pain surprises you. When I'm fucking you so hard you forget who you are. You fucking glow. You break like a queen."

God, I wanted to be broken. Shattered. I wanted him to rip everything from me because I trusted him and I knew he'd put me back together.

"Do it all," I cried.

He got back on his knees and flipped me onto my side, draping a leg over his shoulder before he re-entered me so hard I wept anew. He stuck three fingers in my mouth and put his palm under my chin, driving my head back until all I could see of him was the shape of his body bound to mine in the shadow.

"There's so much I'm going to do to you." He growled the threat with my spit on his fingers. "And you're going to take it."

He was deep, rubbing my clit and my spanked ass with his body, swirling pain and pleasure together in a whirl. Consciousness at the deep end funneling away into submission.

"Come, baby. Come."

I came, crooning around his fingers. All the pain surrendered to the pleasure of his will.

———————

CADEN HELD me for a long time. A cloud-like fatigue had taken me over. I was conscious but enervated, like a woman on a strong opiate. The pain was gone, leaving behind a deep satisfaction. He stroked me in that way he did, absently running his fingers over my face and body in silence.

I wasn't much of a lotion person. Caden searched the bags I hadn't unpacked yet and found Vaseline to rub on my bottom.

He inspected my skin for damage, kissing my lower back. "You'll be fine by tomorrow afternoon."

My half sleep drained away, leaving space for a soft tug on the string between us. "Stay."

He lay next to me and stroked my arm like an artist appreciating his work. The room was dark and warm. Crickets chirped outside. The world was far away, and we were cocooned in moonlight and warmth.

"I have an hour to get back."

An hour was nothing. A blip. I knew better than to demand more. He took his obligations seriously. If I asked for more, I'd become a responsibility and he'd be torn between the two. I didn't want to do that to him.

"Was it all right?" I asked.

He didn't answer right away, and in my passive state, I didn't worry that he'd tell me he'd been uncomfortable or disengaged. His response didn't matter as long as it was honest. He and I were made of a single solid mass that could not be separated.

"I should ask you that."

"I'll tell you." I got up on one elbow. "But I want you to say first."

He shifted to get on his back, and I bent over him. Light from the night sky caught his eye, draining the color to the cast of the moon.

"I fell right into it," he said, looking out the window. "This kind of detachment. When you cried, I liked it. Part of me was hoping you'd tell me to stop, but even that part was happy you wouldn't." He looked back at me and touched my cheek. "It wasn't the same though. It wasn't split apart. It was normal doubting. But Grey?" He held my face still as if he wanted to aim his words at my brain and he was more likely to hit the bullseye if I couldn't move. "I can live without it. I don't have to do that anymore if you don't want me to."

I kissed him. "It's totally hot."

"Are you sure?"

I put my head on his chest, and he ran his fingers through my hair. Facing the window, the spotlight of the full moon was setting over the cinderblock wall and birds perched on the barbed wire.

"Can I tell you something weird and gross?" I asked.

"Of course."

"Will you still love me?"

"Nope."

His answer only highlighted the stupidity of the question. My husband had no time for bullshit.

"When I was a girl," I said, "I used to have fantasies about being injured in the forest. I got there different ways. Didn't matter. I was in a big forest, alone and desperate. A man would find me and take me back to his cabin. He'd demand sex before he gave me first aid or a splint or whatever it was. Sometimes he was nice, and sometimes he wasn't. I know that's rapey and weird, but it turned me on... this idea I could give someone my pain." I lifted myself up so I could look at him. "And the thing was, I couldn't ask for that from anyone. I never trusted a man enough. I couldn't even ask you, but it was like a part of you knew."

He considered the curves of my face, tracing them silently.

"I don't want to be thankful this happened," I said.

"We would have gotten here eventually." He pulled my leg over him from behind my knee until I straddled him.

He was hard and thick under me, and I slid along the length of him.

"When we were ninety."

"Baby," he croaked like an old man, reaching between us, "bend over your walker so I can hit you with my cane."

When I laughed, I raised my body a little, and he got his cock against my opening.

"Oh, honey," I made a sad attempt at an old woman voice, "I can't feel it through my diapers."

We laughed, and I pushed down until he entered my sore, wet pussy. I moved over him as he ran his hands over my ribs and breasts.

"It'll be just like that," he said. "Old as dirt and still fucking. You and me."

"You and me."

We fucked like a sweet couple with nothing but happiness in front of us.

Chapter Twenty-Two

CADEN

I felt great. For the first time since I'd first felt Damon's hiss or the nameless buzz, I felt truly whole. Six days went by with neither a relapse nor the threat of one. I went on a medevac, and though the heights still bothered me, I did my job and came back without a voice or a sound or an errant perception.

"You seem weirdly happy," Boner said over Thursday beers on the roof.

"It makes me uncomfortable, gotta be honest," Stoneface added.

"My wife." I shrugged. "What can I say?"

"Thanks for the mental images," Boner said, tipping his bottle to me in mock appreciation.

The evening prayer call arced over the city as soon as the sun dipped below the horizon.

"So," Stoneface asked, "what's she doing exactly?"

"That, my friend, is none of your business."

Agent Orange laughed. Boner shook his head. Heartland was on duty, but he would have changed the subject.

"Nah, I mean... here. What's that shot she's doling out?"

I sipped my beer. That wasn't any of his business either. Blackthorne had worked out a permissions system that didn't exactly override army medical, but since it was through the DoD, it didn't give them the authority to ask specific questions.

"I don't know," I lied, focusing on a grain of truth. I wanted out of the conversation.

"I'm asking because it's the fucked-up-in-the-head guys who get it."

As usual, I couldn't get a read on what he was thinking.

"And when they do, it's like..." Agent Orange spread out his hands. "Pow. They're cured."

"*If* they get it," Stoneface said. "Some don't. Some she doesn't do anything with."

"I noticed that," Agent Orange added. Him I could read. He wasn't accusatory. Not exactly. He was holding his judgment, but the judgment was getting loose.

"Guys, she works for Blackthorne. Who the fuck knows

what they do? It's not like she tells me. She's got NDAs up the ass."

"That shot though." Stoneface shook his head.

"Fucking miracle," Boner added.

"Well," I said before finishing my beer, "I guess she's just magic."

"THEY'RE TALKING," I said to Greyson a few days after the rooftop beers.

We'd had a dozen casualties come in overnight, and one had been flagged for the Blackthorne psych. Everyone had watched as she spoke to the guy, and when she didn't give him the shot, they dispersed like a crowd after the firetrucks left. I caught her outside the hospital before she got back on the truck to the offices.

"Why?" she asked. "Because we haven't spent a night together in over a week?"

It had been busy, and our schedules hadn't overlapped. It sucked, but that wasn't what I was talking about.

"About your miracle shots."

In the desert wind, her hair crossed her face like a web. "It's not a miracle. It's research and preparation." She faced into the gust to clear the hair out of her eyes.

"They don't know why some people are getting it and not others. Or if it's going to contraindicate anything they're prescribing."

"I'll tell my boss. It may be something PR has to handle."

An errant strand crossed her face, sticking to her bottom lip. We didn't touch or show affection publicly, but I moved it without thinking.

"I miss you," she said.

The whoosh of the wind almost drowned her out. We stood in broad daylight, surrounded by people walking in and out of the hospital. But we were totally alone.

"What happens if I slip back?" I said.

"Back?"

"If I crack. If the split comes again."

Her brow knotted. "I don't think that's going to happen."

"How do you know?"

She shook her head slightly, slowly, thinking about her answer just a little too fucking hard.

"You don't know," I said.

"It's hard to explain."

"Try me."

She looked around, checking for ears and eyes. I led her to a window ledge wide enough to sit on.

She pulled the hair off her face and took a deep breath. "You're in a group that developed dissociative disorder because you had previous trauma. You're the only one who had a chance to relive the event while being talked through it. You faced your fear and got control. You're the only one who's been made whole."

I waited for more. Some proof. Some studies. Some evidence that it wasn't coming back. I got none of that. All I got was a look of devotion, which was nice but no cure for my concern.

"So, you don't know shit."

"No. Not really. But, Caden..." She reached for me, but I didn't return the affection.

"I don't know how I ever lived like that," I said. "If it comes back, I don't know what I'll be. Loving you isn't going to be enough to fix it, and I can't do it again. I won't."

What was I threatening exactly?

It didn't matter. I'd fought enemies I couldn't see because they were inside me. The memory of the splits, the constant battles, the lack of sleep, the torment of feeling that there was something hostile I couldn't escape was too much.

"I know you're scared."

"If I slip back, will you give it to me? The shot? Will I get it?"

"You're not going to slip back."

"I'm not playing this game with you. Yes or no?"

Through the veil of hair whipping over her face, I held her eyes with mine. The wind took on a rhythm that got louder and louder. I wouldn't move until she answered.

The rhythm turned into the *thup-thup-thup* of choppers. Paramedics ran out to meet new casualties. I'd be managing life and limb in minutes.

"Grey," I said urgently.

"There's a dose with your name on it."

Was that enough reassurance? I decided it was.

"Thank you," I said in an exhale of relief.

Chapter Twenty-Three

Standing in front of the medical refrigerator, I held his syringe.

CADEN ST. JOHN
145-361-9274

To be given soon after an event as described in section 54a.
Breathing methodology B2.

A PLACEBO, right?

Like Yarrow's.

Supposedly.

He had to medevac like everyone else. He was exposed to traumatic situations every few days. Which one would tip him? Which one would shut him down or split him apart? Was this a cure for a man who was whole? Or a detonator for an unprotected mind?

"Lunch?"

I jumped. Ronin peered in from the hall.

"You scared me." I put the syringe back.

"What are you looking at?"

"Just... dosages. Making sure we're consistent."

"We're not. They're different for everyone depending on height, weight, gender, how long we treated them stateside." He pointed at the ceiling, the sky, or the cafeteria. "I hear they have tuna sandwiches."

"They always have tuna sandwiches."

"So, the rumors are true."

I walked up to the top floor with him. The elevator was broken so frequently and was so slow when it wasn't that everyone just took the stairs.

When we were alone, I broached what Caden had told me the day before. "The medical staff is asking what the shots are about. How are they supposed to be sure it won't react negatively with something they're administering?"

"Legitimate concern, but we covered it in trials."

"Why everyone who needs it isn't getting it."

He shot out a derisive laugh. "Try giving it to someone who hasn't had the prep and see what happens."

"What happens?"

"Usually nothing." He held open the cafeteria door for me. "Usually."

NIGHT.

Caden and I on his narrow bed, bodies draped over each other. His chest rising and falling under my head. The beating of his heart. His fingers drifting over my shoulder as the doors of my mind clicked gently shut, one by one, in surrender to sleep.

I knew the sound of choppers overhead. I could hear them from miles away. I could tell if they were going to land on the north pad or by the hospital. I could tell a Blackhawk from an Osprey, speeding to save lives from a standard landing.

Caden's hand stopped moving just before I heard it. Blackhawk. If it came from the south, it was going to the airfield. If it came from the west, it was touching down on the hospital landing pad.

We remained twisted together, frozen as the *thup-thups* got louder, our full attention on the sky.

THE DAY HAD STARTED NORMALLY, but the insurgents had had a different plan. I overheard the soldiers and marines as they came in. US positions had been hit on four fronts. Massive casualties.

In Balad, I could have helped. If no one needed a psychiatrist, I could push paper, carry containers, take orders.

In Baghdad, I felt useless. Men were coming in torn apart, bloody, screaming for their buddies, and I couldn't help. Couldn't even talk to them until a doctor found a flagged file. Then Dana would come with the BiCam and I'd have a purpose.

I went to the chow hall to get out of the way and found Dana at a table with a cup of coffee and a gossip magazine.

"Hey," she said.

"What are you reading?" I sat down.

"Anna Nicole Smith died. So sad."

"Yeah, that's terrible. Aren't you supposed to be waiting at the office until they open a flagged file?"

"I brought everything," she said, tapping something between her legs. I looked under the table. It was a big medical cooler. "She was thirty-nine. Overdose."

"Yeah." I blew on my coffee. It looked like Dana didn't have the kind of gossip I was hoping for. "How's everything with Mr. Trona?"

She flipped a page, eyes still on the magazine. "Went on a security detail two days ago."

"I'm sure he's fine."

"He was on the run that was ambushed this morning."

"I'm so sorry," I said. "I didn't know he was part of that."

"Did you know Anna Nicole Smith dropped out of school at fourteen?"

"Yeah. I mean, no." I went from agreement to honesty in four words. A teardrop fell onto her magazine, leaving a dark-gray burst. "Do you want to go check the hospital? See if he came back?"

I handed her a tissue. She took it without looking up.

"There's still no word." She turned the page. "But I'm sure they're going to be fine once they get a medevac in."

"The medevacs have been back and forth. Maybe he's back."

"Nothing's gone out since the one that got shot down."

She did have the gossip I was looking for but not what I'd been hoping for.

There was no delicate way of asking if there had been a doctor on the medevac or if that doctor was my husband. Worry hardened over my confidence, crystalizing like ice on the window as Dana commented on every page of the magazine to distract herself.

Had Caden been on that Blackhawk?

I was cold and brittle, useless to Dana or anyone.

He wouldn't have gone up with casualties coming in. Even if they'd had an injury they needed a surgeon for, they couldn't possibly have spared him. Right?

He'd just been made whole again. God wouldn't take him away so soon after, would he?

The building trembled in answer to my question. The helicopter pad was above us, and something was coming or going. I leaned to look out the window. A Blackhawk with a big red cross on the tail sped across the sapphire sky.

My beeper went off.

"We're on," I said. "I'll help you with the cooler."

"FUCKING NIGHTMARE," DeLeon said to a nurse as she passed. Dana and I carried the cooler between us.

"Wifey," she barked, peeling off the nurse and redirecting herself toward me.

I stopped short, jerking Dana to a stumble.

"You have three flagged on their way." DeLeon softened. "It was a rough ride. They're going to need you."

"Wait!" I called before she could turn her back on me.

"You're asking about him," she said.

"I am."

"I don't have time to give you a hug and a pat on the back."

"I know."

"Four hours ago." Her voice was flat and emotionless. Just the facts. "The medevac he was on was shot down over an active zone. We have reports of multiple fatalities and casualties, military and civilian, including chemical burns."

"Is he—"

"He's not dead, far as we know." A nurse pulled her away, but she called back, "Keep it together, Wifey. We need you."

———

TRONA WAS one of the first off the medevac. Third-degree burns from his right shoulder to his fingertips. Right behind him, children came without their mothers. Soldiers with uniforms burned off. Paramedics with blood drained from their faces and cheeks hollowed out as if joy had been sucked from their mouths.

A paramedic left the ER and promptly vomited on the floor.

"I'll get towels," Dana said.

I ran up to him. "Hey," I said, bent over so I could see the long drop of saliva from his profile. "Come sit."

He listened to me. I wasn't an officer without a commission. I wasn't an interloper. My status as a contractor didn't matter to either of us. I could listen to him, and he could distract me from worrying about Caden.

"It was so fast," he said. "One minute we're landing; the next, we're crashing. Me and the doc get out and we don't know what to do first."

The doc must have been Caden. I didn't react. At least I tried not to.

"I take the guys on the Phrog, and he goes into the street. Got shot at almost right away."

I clutched the fingers of my left hand in my right so tightly my ring pressed against my pinkie.

"But he tripped over this woman..." He took a deep breath in an attempt to keep it together. "Saved his life, but she was..." He shook his head.

"And you?" I said.

"She was melted."

I let him see it in his mind for a few seconds before steering him back. "You took care of the pilot and copilot?"

"Yeah. And two other medics. All fine. Not bad. Minor shit. But we were stuck. All of us. And it was..." He shook his head instead of using words.

"Greyson!" Dana called. She waved me toward the ICU. "Pfc. Karlson's in recovery."

"He was one of mine!" the paramedic exclaimed. "I pulled him out! Is he all right?"

"They don't put dead men in ICU," I said.

"Go find out!" He practically pushed me off my chair. "Then let me know."

He was suddenly like a kid, and I was suddenly carrying the weight of Caden's absence.

"The doctor," I said before walking away. "Is he all right?"

"He was when we left him."

They'd left him there, probably to make room on the

Blackhawk.

I followed Dana into the ICU. She had the shot on a tray by Karlson's bed.

I put on my game face.

If Caden was dead, I'd know from the way the sky shattered.

Chapter Twenty-Four

CADEN

I agreed to land under fire because I was there to get people off the ground, not run back to the Green Zone with my tail between my legs. And yeah, I was terrified. I'd imagined, more than most people, falling out of the sky. It was number one on the list of ways I didn't want to die.

But I'd medevaced dozens of times. Every time I went up, it got easier.

We were circling around a freeway with a hole in the center and debris at the edges. I couldn't say how close to the ground we were when we were hit, but my stomach had already flipped from the descent, then we started spinning.

It wasn't anything like I'd thought it would be. I'd always imagined the fall would be quiet and empty, with nothing but my thoughts and regrets. But it was loud. Centrifugal force pulled me against my seat, and I didn't have an inward-looking thought in my head. I heard and understood the pilot's mayday call. I saw the paramedics with utter clarity and noted that the instruments were all strapped down. I was as lucid as I'd always feared, but I was not afraid. My brain was too busy.

The Blackhawk screwed itself into the ground not far from the hole in the freeway, bending and creaking as a billion dollars in metal bowed around me. The prop smacked into the dirt, creating a ditch.

Then it stopped.

Arms. Legs. Fingers. Toes. Eyes. I took inventory of my body and senses. I was sideways. My ears buzzed, but it wasn't a discrete anger roaring to break free. It was just my ears.

"Doc?" A paramedic leaned over me. Frankie Beans. I knew him. Soft face. Brave heart.

"I'm good." I pressed the buckle of my belt and shrugged off the straps. Frankie helped. I moved slowly in case I had a break I couldn't feel. I'd ache in the morning for sure. "Who's hurt?"

"Unger took a hit to the head."

"No vital organs," I joked, crawling across the cracked space to what had been the front.

"Fuck you," Unger, the copilot, said. Blood covered his face, and his temporal vein was still gushing.

"Everybody out!" our pilot shouted. "Move!"

He shoved paramedic Mari Barron out his window, handing her box of supplies out behind her. Frankie was already putting pressure on Unger's head.

"Doc!" the pilot shouted. "You! Now!"

I grabbed my case and let him push me out.

I WAS JUST A GUY, not fearless, and I was no hero. But I was pretty good at my job under pressure. Everything narrowed down into tight focus. I made the decisions I was supposed to make and let the warriors do the rest. The wounded and the medical staff were put in a concrete bunker with stripped electrical circuits on one wall that used to route power to the highway's lights. I took care of men, children, and women—Iraqi, American, and one Australian.

"Trona," I said, leaning over the contractor. He'd taken a bullet in the arm. Clean exit. "Didn't expect to see you on the job."

"After a building fell on you, I didn't expect to see you ever."

The paramedics had cleaned him up. I started on the sutures. "We have a way of living through stuff, I guess. This is going to hurt."

"More than it already does?"

"Probably not. But you'll throw a football again."

"They were everywhere," he said as I worked. "I never saw anything like it. Benito got his head blown off right in front of me."

That would explain the blobs of green-gray on the front of his shirt.

"We're going to get you back," I said.

"It was quiet," he said. "We avoided Route Irish. I thought—" He cut himself off as I finished up.

"You thought you were safe."

He shook his head quickly. "Never safe, right?"

"Sometimes you're safe."

"I have to get Dana out of here."

"I know how you feel, man. I know how you feel." I took an extra second with my hand on his arm. I had nothing to offer him but that time.

As I got up, a sniper bullet grazed my back. It burned.

"Doc!" Trona yelled.

Mari scrambled over to me as I crouched.

"I'm fine."

"You've got to stay low." Mari checked me out, ripping open the back of my shirt. "This is going to hurt."

"She said."

"Jesus Christ," she mumbled as she checked the wound. "He missed your vertebra by a quarter inch."

"Easier to miss it than to hit it, right, Trona?"

"Right," he grunted. "When are they coming?"

The light from the tiny square window had gotten long and bright as day waned. A medevac wouldn't land under fire a second time.

"Soon," I lied. "They'll pick you up soon."

"I'm not worried about me," he said, gritting his teeth against pain. "I don't want them shooting you, bro. We need you."

THE FIRST MEDEVAC landed just before midnight. Mari and I stayed behind to fit in more wounded.

I didn't know what was going on outside the little cinderblock building, but it was quiet for long stretches leading up to a string of *pop-crack-pop*, then more silence. I had blood and dirt all over me. The room stank of bodily fluids, gunpowder, and flesh.

In the middle of the night, looking at the sky through the

glassless window, I'd gotten lost in what some might have considered prayer.

I'd thanked the capital-U Universe for letting me be there to help, for letting me live, for the men who protected me so I could patch people up.

I'd thanked it for my clarity of mind. The end of the buzz of anger and the hum of cowardice. I was whole, and for that, I counted the stars in Orion's belt and thanked them for Greyson. I could die in an hour, but I'd die myself as one man, one unconflicted consciousness.

The moans of the wounded mixed with the high-pitched creak of crickets just as the *thup-thup* of a medevac came over the horizon. We mobilized everyone to move.

Trona got up on his own and flicked a piece of Benito's brain off a front button.

I had a young boy, about the same age as my *qunbula* kid, with an exploded foot. When they'd brought him to me, I'd frozen for a second with the memory but had shaken myself out of it.

Not the same kid. Obviously.

"Don't go," he said with panicked eyes as the helicopter landed. Decoding the Arabic took a second.

"I bring you." I was sure I'd gotten it wrong, maybe telling him he was bringing me, but he understood well enough to calm down.

"Doc," Mari called, helping a man with an open wound for a leg onto a stretcher, "we're out."

I picked up the kid with the shattered foot and carried him to the medevac. Shots were fired. I kept running, looking straight ahead, and fell.

Chapter Twenty-Five

GREYSON

It was three in the morning. We were in a lull created by the fact that we couldn't get a medevac out to pick up the last of the wounded and two medical staff. One of whom was my husband.

The hardest thing I'd ever done was sit still in that hospital. Especially since I knew he wasn't that far away. Especially since I had working legs and feet. I couldn't do a damn thing, really. I'd never get there before they could send a medevac out, and leaving would make it all worse. Logically, I was exactly where I needed to be.

Yet I felt a physical pull toward him. When I went outside to get air, I saw the three bright stars of Orion's belt. Caden was under the same sky, and he was looking with me. He was my blue sky, my clear day, the protective shell over my world. At night, we were strung together by the stars.

"How's Karlson?" Ronin stood next to me, steamed and pressed, looking at the sky as if trying to figure out what I saw.

The beating of helicopter wings rose above us. It wasn't the first time I'd hoped it was a medevac going out for Caden. I'd given up on hope in favor of trust that he'd be back.

"Fine," I said. "And Humbert. Yarrow's the only one who fell apart."

"Good, good."

The helicopter took off, a black mass blotting out the dots of light and disappearing like hope.

"They're going to get the last of them," Ronin said.

"Thank you," I said to the stars.

"Past two days were like Balad Lite." He shook a cigarette out of a pack and offered me one.

I took my eyes off the sky to decline the smoke. "We didn't even know what we were looking at then when it came to mental trauma."

"Fuck, we didn't." He lit up. "We knew from Vietnam. Korea. But they weren't real soldiers, right? We kicked them out and didn't treat them. We pretended trauma was for pussies. Real men bucked up and went back onto the field. Played the game and won."

It was his turn to look pensively into the sky.

"What's your deal, Ronin? You're a callous asshole except when you're not."

He shrugged and blew out a cone of smoke. "I've seen things I never want to see again, and I didn't do shit. Didn't say shit." He tapped his ash. A single bright ember curled away in the wind and vanished. "You should have come to Abu Ghraib. You would have said something." He took a pull of his cigarette. "You would have saved me."

"And going up there would have destroyed me."

Smoke came from his lips when he laughed. "You? Nah." He stamped out his butt. "Nothing breaks you."

I looked at the night sky, waiting for the one man who made Ronin wrong. "Did you have PTSD from Abu Ghraib?"

"I'm just trying to balance the scales."

"How noble." I wrapped my sweater around my chest against the coldest part of the desert night.

"And futile."

"I'm going to wait inside."

He turned to walk with me, opening the door so I could pass.

"This was a shitstorm," he said. "It'll be a good time to give Caden his shot."

"No fucking way." I went through without looking back.

He caught up to me in front of the reception desk. "Don't you want to know?"

"If he's going to collapse in a heap like Leslie Yarrow? No, I don't want to know."

"It's a placebo."

"Is it?"

"Yes."

"Then let me set up a saline shot with my own hands."

"Do you not get how research works?"

I stood with my legs apart and my arms crossed. "No. At this point, I don't."

He lowered his voice. "This has been a traumatic trip for him. It's the perfect time. We need to show we had consistent treatments for both of them so we can isolate the cause of her breakdown. That's how we determine—"

"Blah blah blah. No. I'm not going to be responsible for breaking him."

I walked away before I had to hear more bullshit reasons.

He wasn't putting Caden in danger. Period. We'd worked too hard to throw it all away.

I WAS on the roof when the medevac landed. Caden had been over the wire many times since he'd treated a pregnant woman in a closet in Fallujah. Still, I half expected him to get off in a fugue and go to his room with his legs and arms drooping with paresis. But he was on his feet, shouting vitals and instructions.

Small things. I thanked the night sky and the rising sun for small things.

WE'D MET in a Balad Air Base scrub room. He'd been undressed and obnoxious. I'd been impressed with the least impressive things about him.

In Baghdad, I couldn't wait to see him. I went into the scrub room again. He was naked from the waist up as a nurse helped him change from a blood-spattered shirt into clean scrubs.

"Caden." I stood at the door. "I was so worried."

"For nothing," he said, getting his hands under the faucet. "You know I wouldn't die without asking permission first."

His next step was soap, but he kept his hands still under the faucet. I wove through the rushing surgical staff to stand by him.

His hands were shaking.

"Shit," he muttered. "Stoney!"

"Yo," Stoneface said through his mask. He was already scrubbed in. When he saw Caden's hands, he nodded. "I got this."

Caden shut the water and walked out. I ran after him, silently walking next to him until we were in a quiet hallway with a window at the end. He stopped and leaned against the wall.

"I thought I was dead," he said, looking at the hands that had betrayed him. His fingers still quaked as if they wanted to run away from his arm.

I slid my hands into his, squeezing as if I could keep them still.

"You're not."

"They were shooting at us and I tripped. I thought..." He took his eyes off his hands and met my gaze. "All the things we haven't done, it was all my fault for coming. I was leaving you alone. I wanted to have kids, and we never did. I could see them in my mind, and I was so sorry."

"It's okay."

"I can still see them."

"Are they cute?"

He laid his lips on my cheek for long seconds, breathing deeply. I felt connected to him by that breath. It was made of steel cables, connecting us near or far.

"They look like you," he said.

"I'm still with you. And if you're fine... I'll tell Ronin you're okay because he's going to ask you to get the BiCam shot."

"I saw Dana before I scrubbed in." He took his face from mine with a shrug. "I told her I'd take it."

The squiggle of the blood streak leading to Leslie Yarrow appeared in front of my eyes. It was the path her head had taken across the room as she was dragged while she fought with the chaos in her mind.

"What? Why?" I asked.

"It's the same shit they were giving me in New York. It's fine. It might even be *better*."

The cables didn't fray. Didn't break. But my control was slipping away even as I tried to grasp our connection and pull it tight.

"Can you just not?" I took his hands and tried to reforge our link with a hard gaze. "Just don't take it."

"Do you know something I don't?"

I did. I knew the one thing that would make giving the shot futile, because the thing about placebos was that they were useless if the subject knew. "It's a placebo."

He laughed and kissed me on the lips with a deep sense of appreciation. "Then what's the problem?"

"The problem," I sulked, crossing my arms and lowering my voice, "is Yarrow got this placebo too, and she had a breakdown a few minutes later. So, either the thought of the shot created the reaction—"

"Which you just killed by telling the patient."

"—or it's not a placebo."

His eyes were so intense I nearly melted under their heat. Blue was a cold color associated with ice and distance, but when he directed it my way, it warmed me.

"I'm whole," he said. "Shaken, yes. But whole. Was she?"

I put my hands on his chest, wishing he hadn't put the shirt on before I had a chance to kiss his skin. "No, but—"

"Okay, take it easy." He took my wrists and kissed my palms. "I'm going to finish this treatment with them and be done with it."

He kissed me before I could protest, and there was so much love and trust in that kiss that I let it melt my objections away. I pulled him into me, and he wrapped his arms around my body as if he was afraid I'd run away.

When I felt his erection against me, I groaned into his mouth, lifting my leg over his waist. He pressed his hardness against my damp softness.

"My room," he said, cupping my breast.

"We're not finished talking about this," I said, grinding into him.

"We're going to talk about our life together. I'm going to give you the entire world. We're going to talk about which part you get first."

"You. You're the part I want first."

"Good, because—"

The doors at the end of the hall swung open. Dana appeared with a metal tray, stopping short when she saw us tangled together. "Oh! There you are. I, uh..."

I got both feet on the floor.

"It's fine," Caden said.

"I have to give you this," Dana replied, setting down the tray with a syringe that told stories.

"No—" I started.

"All right." Caden passed her on the way out, stopping long enough to say, "But give her a sedative."

The doors closed behind him.

"I'm not sure he needs it," I said.

"When he came in he looked a little—"

"He doesn't need it!" I shouted.

Ashamed of my tantrum, I went past her to follow my husband.

He was already sitting in the exam room, rolling up his sleeve.

"Caden, listen to me..."

"I'm fine."

Dana came in with her tray and, not wanting to yell again, I clammed up, crossing my arms and wondering how the hell I was going to get him out of this.

She sat next to him and pulled on latex gloves, smiling from ear to ear. "Thank you so much for taking care of Bobby."

"How's he doing?"

They chatted while she swabbed his skin.

I stood over them, remembering slipping on the squiggle of Yarrow's blood on the linoleum, her red face, the heat and depth of her confusion and pain. She screamed with the voice of an abused child. Would he sound like a little boy locked in a cellar when he got the shot?

"Baby?" Caden asked, his voice far away, drowned out by darkness and horror.

I couldn't risk stuffing him back in the bag. Not for his promises or mine.

Dana raised the needle.

"I'll do it." I held out my hand. Momentarily bewildered, Dana froze with the needle between herself and Caden's arm. "It's my responsibility."

"All right," she chirped.

She placed the syringe back on the tray and stood. I sat across from my husband and got gloves on, ready to deliver a death blow to his sanity or a round of nothing at all. Caden leaned forward with a smirk. He liked this. I knew he thought I was sexy with a needle in my hand. After this, he'd fuck me as if it would be the last time he used his dick.

Dana waited impatiently.

Ronin had told me she didn't need a babysitter. Well, neither did I.

"Can you get his paperwork for me?" I asked. "I want to make some notes after I'm done."

She nodded and left.

"You're really sexy when you boss people around," Caden said.

I pressed his arm down to hold it steady, feeling the way the skin gave but the muscle didn't. How complex the structure of his cells and nerves was. How touching him made me realize how fragile he was. How quickly I could lose him.

With my right hand, I held the needle to his arm, holding

his elbow with the left hand. I felt him watching me. His impatience to do this thing so he could get me into bed.

The shot was nothing. Had to be. Ronin would lie, but about this? No. Not about the research.

But he had bosses.

Maybe they lied.

Maybe they'd made a mistake.

Maybe Leslie Yarrow and Caden St. John had become test cases.

"Come on, baby," Caden said. "I want to get moving here."

If I didn't give him the shot, Dana would. Ronin had authorized her to do her job with or without me. And since I'd asked them to send a second syringe? Squirting this one on the floor, if I even could, would just delay the inevitable. When the syringe didn't change color, they'd know I hadn't given it to him. They'd fire me. Send me home. When the new syringe came, Dana would give him the shot he was convinced he could handle.

I was trapped.

Caden was trapped.

The BiCam had to go into someone before Dana returned, and it wasn't going to be Caden.

Quickly, I turned the needle downward.

And away.

The diagonally cut tip turned toward me, the white rubbery hub hungry to turn blue when it touched my skin.

So fast, but carefully, with all my attention on what I was doing, I pushed it into my left bicep, lowering the plunger until the syringe was empty.

Caden leaned back.

"We're done here," I said. By the time I dropped the syringe on the metal tray, the hub was already blue.

HUBRIS IS EXCESSIVE, defiant pride or self-confidence.

That wasn't what this was. I'd given myself the shot out of certainty. Trust. I was sane and whole, so much so that even my fears and quirks confirmed my core mental soundness.

My body had been broken at the wrist, pierced at the sternum, snapped at the collarbone, but nothing could change what I was. Who I was. If you'd asked me if I believed humans had souls, I would have given you arguments about genetics and upbringing that added up to a denial. But I must have believed. When I gave myself that shot, it was because I trusted that I had a sane, unbreakable core. I was confirming the unconfirmable.

I believed in my soul. I believed it would never change. I believed that to protect Caden, I'd be able to shrug off whatever confusion this stuff created.

My attention was locked on Caden as he leaned back with his sleeve rolled up and the alcohol drying on his arm. His focus further established what I already knew. I was safe.

"Why?" was all he said.

"It's for the best." I stood, suddenly uncomfortable with inaction.

I had to move forward. Whatever that was, it was a direction. My heart pounded with anxiety. I felt trapped in an inert state that would corrode me. It wasn't an overwhelming feeling. It was more like an irritation. An itch on the sole of your foot in otherwise comfortable shoes. Definitely within the normal range.

I walked out. Forward into the lobby and outside, where dawn broke the blackness of the sky into blues. He was right behind me. I knew it without hearing him.

But I had to keep moving. I didn't even know where I was going except forward to an undefinable destination.

He grabbed my arm. "Slow down."

I stopped long enough for him to wrap his arms around me. I was locked in a stillness that was comfortable because it was him. "I'm sorry. I just got claustrophobic all of a sudden."

"Why did you do that?"

"I don't want you to have the serum or a placebo or anything. I don't care about the research, and I don't care what they say about what's in it. I don't want to risk it. Period. That's my professional assessment."

He ran his thumb over my cheek with that perfect casual pressure. His touch grounded me to the moment, soothing the itch to move.

"Okay," he said. "Are you going to be all right?"

"Yes." I ran my finger along the edge of his placket. "Now I am." The world was inside the spaces where we touched. Nothing could break us. Nothing.

"If the shot wasn't a placebo?"

"I'll be fine."

"Are you sure?" He lifted my chin so I could look at him. Behind him, the sky was lightening to the exact color of the eyes that saw right through me.

"Yes." I was five miles off the ground in his gaze.

"Greyson?"

"I'm fine."

"If you're not, I'll kill him." He meant Ronin, but I was fine. "I'll burn Blackthorne down. Do you understand me?"

"Yes." My voice was barely a whisper. I understood. He was forward motion and stillness. His eyes were the lock of gravity under a sky that melted, moved, shifted, cracked.

Behind his still points of blue, the sky was rent into two distinct halves, and the trust that my soul could bear anything shattered with it.

It was not a placebo.

TO BE CONTINUED
Get *Over the Edge* today!

The Edge Series is four books.

Rough Edge | *On The Edge* | *Broken Edge* | *Over the Edge*

CHECK YOUR FAVORITE RETAILER FOR THE
FREE PREQUEL
—— *CUTTING EDGE* ——

FOLLOW ME ON FACEBOOK, Twitter, Instagram, Tumblr or Pinterest.

Join my fan groups on Facebook and Goodreads.

Get on the mailing list for deals, sales, new releases and bonus content - JOIN HERE.

My website is cdreiss.com

Chapter Twenty-Six

GREYSON

I had to move forward. Whatever that was, it was a direction. My heart pounded with anxiety. I felt trapped in an inert state that would corrode me. It wasn't an overwhelming feeling. It was more like an irritation. An itch on the sole of your foot in otherwise comfortable shoes. Definitely within the normal range.

I walked out. Forward into the lobby and outside, where dawn broke the blackness of the sky into blues. He was right behind me. I knew it without hearing him.

But I had to keep moving. I didn't even know where I was going except forward to an undefinable destination.

He grabbed my arm. "Slow down."

I stopped long enough for him to wrap his arms around me. I was locked in a stillness that was comfortable because it was him. "I'm sorry. I just got claustrophobic all of a sudden."

"Why did you do that?"

"I don't want you to have the serum or a placebo or anything. I don't care about the research, and I don't care what they say about what's in it. I don't want to risk it. Period. That's my professional assessment."

He ran his thumb over my cheek with that perfect casual pressure. His touch grounded me to the moment, soothing the itch to move.

"Okay," he said. "Are you going to be all right?"

"Yes." I ran my finger along the edge of his placket. "Now I am." The world was inside the spaces where we touched. Nothing could break us. Nothing.

"If the shot wasn't a placebo?"

"I'll be fine."

"Are you sure?" He lifted my chin so I could look at him. Behind him, the sky was lightening to the exact color of the eyes that saw right through me.

"Yes." I was five miles off the ground in his gaze.

"Greyson?"

"I'm fine."

"If you're not, I'll kill him." He meant Ronin, but I was fine. "I'll burn Blackthorne down. Do you understand me?"

"Yes." My voice was barely a whisper. I understood. He was forward motion and stillness. His eyes were the lock of gravity under a sky that melted, moved, shifted, cracked.

Behind his still points of blue, the sky was rent into two distinct halves, and the trust that my soul could bear anything shattered with it.

It was not a placebo.

TO BE CONTINUED
Get *On The Edge* today!

The Edge Series is four books.

Rough Edge | *On The Edge* | *Broken Edge* | *Over the Edge*

CHECK YOUR FAVORITE RETAILER FOR THE
FREE PREQUEL
—— *CUTTING EDGE* ——

FOLLOW ME ON FACEBOOK, Twitter, Instagram, Tumblr or Pinterest.

Join my fan groups on Facebook and Goodreads.

Get on the mailing list for deals, sales, new releases and bonus content - JOIN HERE.

My website is cdreiss.com

The Edge Series

Rough. Edgy. Sexy enough to melt your device.

Cutting Edge | Rough Edge | On The Edge | Broken Edge | Over the Edge

The Games Duet

Adam Steinbeck will give his wife a divorce on one condition. She join him in a remote cabin for 30 days, submitting to his sexual dominance.

Marriage Games | Separation Games

The Submission Series

Jonathan brings out Monica's natural submissive.

Submission | Domination | Connection

Corruption Series

Their passion will set the Los Angeles mafia on fire.

SPIN | RUIN | RULE

Forbidden Series

Fiona has 72 hours to prove she isn't insane. Her therapist has to get through three days without falling for her.

| USE | BREAK

Contemporary Romances

ood and sports romances for the sweet and sexy romantic.

Shuttergirl | Hardball | Bombshell | Bodyguard

Made in the USA
Middletown, DE
08 July 2018